Daniel stepped from the shower into the steam....

He grabbed a towel and wrapped it around his damp body. He was happy to have remained in hiding long enough to try to wash away the odd, heated sensitivity that covered his skin—although it hadn't worked. Maybe shaving would wake him.

The bathroom mirror was completely fogged. He reached out and rubbed the condensation from its surface. And then rubbed again.

There was no reflection in the mirror.

There'd been a phrase he'd read long ago, in some melodramatic novel. Something about one's blood running cold. Suddenly he knew exactly what it meant. He slammed the bathroom door open, then headed for the bedroom and the mirror over his dresser.

Nothing.

"Uh-oh," he murmured, utterly fascinated. "I'm invisible."

Dear Reader,

You're about to meet one of the most mysterious, magical men!

Dr. Daniel Crompton is many things, but none of them is ordinary, as Suzanna Molloy—and you—are about to find out.

And neither are any of the four heroes in American Romance's new MORE THAN MEN series. Whether their extraordinary powers enable them to grant you three wishes, communicate with dolphins or live forever, their greatest power is that of seduction.

So turn the page—and be seduced by Dr. Daniel Crompton.

It's an experience you'll never forget.

Regards,

Debra Matteucci
Senior Editor and Editorial Coordinator

Anne Stuart

CINDERMAN

Harlequin Books

TORONTO • NEW YORK • LONDON
AMSTERDAM • PARIS • SYDNEY • HAMBURG
STOCKHOLM • ATHENS • TOKYO • MILAN
MADRID • WARSAW • BUDAPEST • AUCKLAND

ISBN 0-373-16525-0

CINDERMAN

Chapter One

Nancy Drew, she wasn't. She was a far cry from Brenda Starr, as well. Slinking through the sterile corridors of Beebe Control Systems International, her head down, her eyes focused on her battered sneakers, Suzanna Molloy could feel her heart pounding, her adrenaline pumping, her brain going into overdrive. Maybe she wasn't cut out for undercover work.

If anyone recognized her, she would be in very deep dog droppings. She was persona non grata around here, having been impertinent enough to ask questions about the corporate structure and political affiliations of the mysterious megacorporation that had sprung up out of nowhere in the last few years, and having compounded her crime by asking those questions in print. Not that a huge multinational complex like BBCSI should be threatened by the small trade newspaper she worked for. After all, the *Tech-Sentinel* had an excellent reputation for hard-nosed reporting in the scientific field, but that field was, in fact, quite small. BBCSI could squash the *Tech-Sentinel* flat, if they wanted. And if they made the mistake of thinking no one would notice.

So far, they'd been smart enough to do no more than offer a few warnings, and to refuse to grant Suzanna any interviews. But she wasn't the mild-mannered sort that took rejection lightly. Not when she had hints of exactly what Dr. Daniel Crompton was working on.

Now she huddled into an oversize lab coat, reminding herself that she needed to walk like a dweeb. Keep her head down, shuffle her feet, maybe even mumble underneath her breath. She'd spent enough of her life among the computer nerds and scientific misfits to be able to pass herself off as one. Just long enough to get herself into Crompton's private lab. The lab that no one, not even his bosses or assistants, was allowed to enter.

Suzanna Molloy hadn't gotten where she was by taking no for an answer, she thought, darting a surreptitious glance down the hall. Not that she'd gotten that far by most standards. A two-room apartment in an old Victorian house on the edge of a northern California town, a bank account that kept her in yogurt and a car that had seen better days did not amount to impressive accomplishments in the scheme of things. But they were things she'd accomplished herself. Everything she had, she'd earned—including her reputation.

She wondered if she'd be quite so determined if it were anyone other than Daniel Crompton. She'd met the great Dr. Crompton on several occasions—all public receptions when the BBCSI hadn't been able to keep the press at bay—and it had hardly been love at first sight. She'd decided early on that Crompton was one of those men whose ego was almost as large as his intellect, and in Crompton's case that was saying a great deal. The man was legendary—for his brilliance, his youth and his chilly manner. The fact that he wasn't half-bad to look at only made him better copy.

She whipped around the corner, breathing a sigh of relief. It had been difficult enough getting past the security guards in the first place. One would have thought BBCSI harked back to cold-war technology, given the almost hysterical level of protection the fortresslike complex boasted. Fortunately she had friends in low places: the picture ID with its computer scan code was meticulous enough to avoid detection, and the blueprint of the building would enable her to make her way to Crompton's fortified third-story lab without any betraying hesitation.

Once she got there, it would be up to her to get inside. She had no illusions. The place would have security that would make Fort Knox seem like a public park, but she wasn't about to give up if she got that far. She had in the capacious pocket of her lab coat a handy-dandy device that would take care of any computer-coded lock. She'd only be in trouble if they went in for something as archaic as a dead bolt and key.

She'd chosen her time well. Even the most dedicated security freaks and scientific geniuses liked to get home to a hot meal, and it was just after five-thirty. Most of the employees were too intent on getting the hell out of the place to notice another white-coated employee, and BBCSI was vast enough for her to simply blend in.

When she reached the third floor, she found it deserted. Crompton must have already gone home, and the computerized lock on his unmarked lab door would be child's play for the circumventor one of her friends at the paper had set up for her. Taking a deep breath, she walked to the door of the lab, listening for a moment.

Not a sound within, and if she could trust her instincts, which she usually could, the place was empty. Doubtless, there were security cameras all over the place, and she moved closer to the door, the white coat shielding her actions as she quickly, efficiently tripped the lock and then stepped inside, closing the heavy door silently behind her.

DR. DANIEL CROMPTON stood inside Henry Osborn's plush inner office, impatient as always.

"For heaven's sake, Dan, have a seat," Osborn said, using his usual boisterous charm, something he'd perfected during his twenty years in the corporate high life.

Daniel was immune to charm. And he hated being called Dan. "I'll stand," he said in his deep voice. "I won't be here long."

Osborn didn't let his irritation show, but Daniel knew he was feeling it. "Hell, Dan, you make me feel like a principal calling a recalcitrant schoolboy onto the carpet."

"That's your problem," Daniel replied with exquisite rudeness.

This time he did manage to ruffle Osborn's cheer. The older man's small eyes darkened for a moment, and then he showed his teeth in a semblance of a smile. "We need results, Dan."

"When I accepted your funding, I did so on my terms." Daniel found this all quite tedious, but then, most of his life outside his lab involved wasting his time with fools like Osborn, and he'd grown inured to it. "You provide the money and leave me alone."

"Yes, but we need something. A sign of progress, of good faith. You know, if it were simply up to me, you'd be left to your own timetable. But we've got a board of directors, stockholders, demanding results. General Armstead has been on my tail for a week now, about you."

Daniel simply shrugged.

Osborn got up and came around the desk. He was a trim man in his early sixties, impeccably dressed, impeccably mannered. He was also a snake and a liar.

He put his hand on Daniel's shoulder and stared up at him earnestly. "You know what we're after. And you're the man to do it. Half the scientists in the world are trying to create cold fusion, but our money's on you. If anyone's going to do it, you will."

Daniel stared at him. "At this point I'm not particularly interested in cold fusion."

"Damn it, how could you not be! I'd heard you've been concentrating your efforts on physical chemistry, and that's going to get you nowhere. The only way you're going to create cold fusion is with lasers, with—"

"If you want to create cold fusion, Osborn, I'm sure you can find space for a lab," Daniel said.

Osborn's hands clenched for a moment, then relaxed. "You know, you're damned annoying, Dan. If you weren't so brilliant, someone would probably wring your neck."

Daniel looked down at him. "They could try."

"We need some results, Dan. At least a preliminary report. I trust you—"

"If you trust me, why do you need a preliminary report?"

"I said *I* trust you. I'm just the lowly CEO. Armstead's head of the board of directors, and after spending thirty years in the army, he's used to having his orders obeyed. Just give us something. Anything."

Daniel considered him for a long moment. He didn't trust him, but then, he didn't trust anyone. Trust was a human emotion and a waste of time, and Daniel Crompton never wasted time. It was too precious a commodity.

He'd already wasted more than enough with this man. "I'll have one of my lab assistants write you a report."

"Your lab assistants don't know diddly. You don't let them anywhere near your experiments, you just keep them glued to computers, running theoretical tests."

"It keeps them busy," he said. "I'll have Jackson do it."

Osborn didn't even blink, something Daniel could respect. Robert Jackson was Osborn's spy and stooge, and they all thought Daniel was too involved in his work to realize it. Daniel didn't trust anyone, but Jackson's yuppie friendliness had made him more suspect than most.

"You know what the stakes are, Dan," Osborn said. "You know what cold fusion could do, I don't need to remind you. Don't you care about providing unlimited, safe energy for the world? Don't you care about ending our reliance on oil-producing nations? Don't you want to help make the world a better place?"

"Not particularly," Daniel said with complete honesty. "I'm only interested in my work."

"Danny—" Osborn began.

"My name is Daniel," he said, ruthlessly interrupting Osborn. *Dan* he could barely tolerate; *Danny* was going beyond the pale. "Or Dr. Crompton, if you prefer. And ask Jackson what I'm doing. I'm sure he can come up with a reasonable guess. For a spy, he's quite intelligent." He turned on his heel and started toward the door.

"I'm not finished," Osborn said, sounding petulant.

Daniel didn't pause. "I am," he said. And he closed the door quietly behind him.

The whole thing was incredibly tedious, he thought as he let himself back into the lab. He was so damned tired of dealing with the corporate mentality. He'd accepted Beebe's offer several years ago for a number of reasons, including the fact that they seemed to have more money and fewer restrictions than anyone else making an offer for his services, and the offers had been plentiful. The government had wanted him, of course, but he'd never been fond of bureaucrats. The defense industry's offer had been tempting, but in the end he decided he disliked generals even more than bureaucrats. Private industry gave him the hives; academia was impoverished. BBCSI had seemed the perfect solution, a young multicorporation whose right hand didn't seem to know what its left hand was doing. Apart from Osborn and the deceptively avuncular General Armstead, they were an innocuous bunch. The corporation was large enough to hand over all its vast resources and leave him alone.

Until the last few months. They searched his lab at least every other day. It was usually Jackson, but sometimes it was one of the other brilliant but completely uncreative research assistants Daniel had been given. He wasn't particularly concerned—there was no way they were going to find what he was working on. They were still convinced he was working on cold fusion, and as long as they were looking in that direction it would take more than all their puny intellects put together to figure out what he was up to.

He'd present his results to Osborn, Armstead and their confederates sooner or later. After all, they'd paid for it. But not before he'd finished with his obsessive checking and rechecking. He'd been able to duplicate the results a half-dozen times. He wasn't about to make his discoveries public until he was convinced, and he needed at least a half-dozen more trials.

He'd been at the computer when Osborn had issued his summons. He headed back in that direction, then stopped. Something wasn't right.

He turned around slowly, surveying the sterile, obsessively neat confines of his spacious lab. He hadn't been working at the hood—that section of the physical lab used for dangerous experiments—for days now, and yet it looked different. There was a definite odor, something burning, and he started toward it, then halted.

"Who the hell are you?"

The intruder had been in the middle of sneaking toward the door. He turned and glared at her as she stood like a deer pinned by a set of headlights. Except there was no fear in her steady gaze.

"Er—I'm new here," she said, sounding embarrassed and innocent. Except that he didn't believe her. "I'm looking for Dr. Smith's lab, and I thought this was it."

"There is no Dr. Smith at BBCSI," he said flatly.

"There has to be. Do you know how many Smiths there are in this country?" she asked.

"No, and I don't care. And you're no lab assistant. I recognize you. You're that reporter. How did you get in here?"

She straightened her shoulders, meeting him glare for glare. He couldn't remember her name—it was something like Samantha—but he remembered that look. He supposed she was pretty enough, if she weren't so damned interfering. He didn't like interfering women. He liked them plump, passive and silent, content to feed him and stroke him and leave him alone when he was working.

Unfortunately he had yet to meet such a paragon, but Samantha or whatever her name was had to be one of the worst.

"I'm not *that reporter*," she said, her voice as cool as his. "I'm Suzanna Molloy. And if you ever agreed to an interview, Dr. Crompton, I wouldn't be forced to go to such extremes to find out exactly what it is you're doing."

"Your curiosity justifies breaking and entering, Ms. Molloy? And just how did you get into Beebe in the first place? Someone must have been helping you."

"I'm not about to reveal my sources, to you or to anyone. I've heard rumors that you're working on cold fusion, Dr. Crompton."

"Just about everyone in my field is working on cold fusion. That isn't news." He moved to the telephone, picking up the receiver and pushing a button.

"What are you doing?"

"Calling security."

"Wait." She moved quickly—gracefully, he had to admit—and disconnected him before the call was made. "Just a few answers, Dr. Crompton. I've heard that there's something very wrong going on here at Beebe. That you're working on something extraordinary, something well beyond cold fusion, and that there's a good chance it might fall into the wrong hands."

He stared down at her. She was tall for a woman, taller than Osborn, and her eyes behind her wire-rimmed glasses were a clear, intelligent brown. Intelligence. He hated that in a woman.

"Where did you get your information?"

"Is it true?" she persisted. "Are you working on cold fusion?"

"No," he said flatly.

"Then it's something even more important. Though I can't imagine what."

"That's the problem with people nowadays, Ms. Molloy," he said. "Not enough imagination."

She had a wide mouth, one that curved in a reluctant smile that he found oddly fascinating. "People usually say reporters have too *much* imagination."

"Don't try to charm me, Molloy," he snapped. "I'm immune."

Her smile vanished as she stared at him in shock. "Charm you?" she echoed. "No one's ever accused me of having charm before."

"Don't expect flattery from me. What were you doing in here?"

"I'm certain you're incapable of flattery, Dr. Crompton," she shot back. "And I was simply observing. I didn't touch anything. Though if I were you, I wouldn't go off and leave an experiment like that."

"What experiment?" The burning smell was stronger now, and all his instincts were on the alert.

"In the hood. I couldn't tell what you were doing—you didn't leave your lab notebook out—but I would think—"

"I wasn't working on anything," he said, whirling around and starting toward the hood, just as smoke began pouring out. It was thick, oily and green, accompanied by a noxious odor.

"Where's the fire extinguisher?" Suzanna Molloy shouted through the fumes. Within seconds, they began to engulf her figure and the room itself.

"Get the hell out of here!" he said, slamming the hood down over the bubbling, roiling mass.

"Where's the fire extinguisher?" she shouted again.

There was no way he could stop the heavy fumes from escaping, no way he could even begin to guess what concoction had been brewed on his bench during his absence. All he could do was get out of there and take Suzanna Molloy with him.

He could barely find her through the swirling darkness. Her body was warm, strong, solid when he bumped up against her, and though she struggled for a moment, he was a great deal stronger than she was, and he simply dragged her over to the door. Only to find it inexplicably locked.

The only other exit to the lab was dangerously near the hood. He heard a sudden roaring sound. "Get down," he shouted, shoving her.

She had the gall to slap him, something he could almost admire, but he shoved her down on the floor, anyway, covering her with his larger body, shielding her, as the force of the explosion rocked the room, shattering the windows and showering them with broken glass and something warm and fetid. For a moment he absorbed the feel of her body beneath him. And then the hot gluey substance began to leak through his clothes, burning his flesh, and he let out a muffled howl of pain.

SUZANNA WAS FLOATING. It was dark, hot and choking, the stink all around her, yet somehow she was safe. His body was pressed down on hers, covering hers, and he was strong, large, keeping her from the evil that surrounded them. She could feel something hot and wet begin to ooze through her clothing, through the jeans and the lab coat, small patches of burning fire, but she couldn't move to brush it away. Crompton was pinning her down.

She put her arms up, to push him away, then drew them back in horror when she realized they were covered with a greenish slime. He was moaning quietly, and through the greasy smoke and darkness she could see that his eyes were closed. He had a cut on his forehead, probably from the flying glass, and blood was pouring down the side of his face.

Distantly she became aware of other things. The brightness of the emergency lights filling the darkness, the sounds of alarms echoing through the complex, the pounding on the locked door. Their bodies were blocking it, and Crompton was too big for her to move, too big for her to crawl out from under him.

She reached up and caught his shoulders, grimacing at the slime that coated her fingers. "Dr. Crompton," she shouted, but her voice came out hoarse and strained from the smoke. "Daniel." She shook him.

He opened his eyes and stared down at her. He looked dazed, almost innocent, and she was suddenly very much aware that he was a man, an attractive man, even bleeding and covered in green slime. Then his eyes focused, his mouth curled in disgust, and he scrambled off her, staggering slightly.

And then he reached down and hauled her to her feet, out of the way, just as the door slammed open.

A moment later they stumbled out into the hallway, assaulted by noise, by voices. Hands were touching her, poking at her, trying to make her lie down, but she wasn't about to lie anywhere, not with all these people milling around, shouting at her. She'd be trampled. She searched through the crowds for Crompton, and for a moment she couldn't spot him. Then she saw him, towering over the others, swaying slightly, his lab coat coated with the same green slime that was burning her skin.

She slapped the restraining hands away and started toward him, through the crowds of people, coming up behind him just as he caught a young man by the lapels of his spotless lab coat and slammed him against the wall. "Jackson," he said, his voice raw with smoke and fury. "What the hell did you do to my lab?"

The man caught in his grip was white-faced with terror and babbling something incoherent. Crompton bounced him off the wall again, and the man collapsed in what appeared to be a faint, just as Suzanna reached him.

"Leave him alone," she said hoarsely. "You've been burned."

He turned to glare down at her, the blood oozing down his face. With his smoke-streaked face, his long hair, the absolute rage in his expression, he looked more like a pirate than a research scientist. "I'm not absolving you," he snarled. "You probably helped set this up, and then it backfired on you. You're in it with them, and it was a damned lucky thing you weren't killed."

"You're crazy," she gasped, rubbing her slime-coated hands down her legs, trying to get some of the burning ooze off her skin.

"Am I?" He reached out for her. His hands were coated with the stuff, as well, and for some reason she thought of old science-fiction movies, and bad colds, and all sorts of other disgusting notions.

She didn't know what he was going to do to her, not with all those witnesses surrounding them. Daniel Crompton didn't seem the type who gave a damn about witnesses, and he was in a truly towering rage. She stared up at him, trying to look pugnacious and failing entirely, as his hands caught her shoulders. Surprisingly enough, they were gentle, not painful.

"Who sent you here?" he demanded. "What were you doing in my lab?" He gave her a small, impatient shake, enough to rattle her already impaired equilibrium. "Are you going to answer my questions?" he demanded, ignoring the BBCSI employees that crowded around him and the paramedics who'd arrived on the scene.

She looked up at him, into his dark, brooding eyes, and that dreamy, spacey place danced over her once more. "Eventually," she murmured. And felt herself begin to slide into a graceful faint.

Chapter Two

Daniel caught her as she fell. His lab was now an inferno, the flames belching forth from the broken door, and he realized if Suzanna Molloy hadn't distracted him, he would be a dead man right now. And he wondered why.

The paramedics took her away from him, and he let her go, noticing at the time that he didn't want to. He filed that unlikely reaction in the back of his brain, to be considered later, as he reluctantly allowed himself to be bundled onto a stretcher. While he had every intention of walking out of the building, of driving himself to the hospital if and when he deemed it necessary, the strength in his legs seemed to give way, and his entire back was burning and throbbing from the green goop that had covered him. Out of the corner of his eye he saw Osborn leaning over Jackson's collapsed form, and there was no mistaking the air of collusion between the two men. Daniel added that to his mental file. He was about to lift his head to look more closely, when he felt the prick of a needle in his arm, too late for him to protest. With one last glance at Suzanna Molloy's unconscious figure on the adjoining gurney, he closed his eyes and went to sleep.

He'd spent some time in pre-med, when he wasn't busy with his other studies. As he lay facedown in the emergency room, while a group of physicians dealt with his back, he decided he was well to be out of that branch of science. For one thing, he didn't seem to have the requisite sadism. They were scrubbing the skin on his back with what felt like steel wool and talking about sports, for God's sake! They assumed he was still knocked out from whatever they'd pumped in his arm, but he had always been resistant to drugs, and he'd regained consciousness just as some helpful female had stripped off what remained of his pants.

"He doesn't look in such bad shape," a female voice observed, while someone took what felt like a razor to his shoulder blades. He didn't move.

"Actually he looks quite luscious," another female said. "What happened to him?"

"Lab explosion," a male voice, the one interested in football, chimed in. "He's in worse shape than the patient in L-4. She only got the stuff on her hands. What do you suppose this junk is?"

"Slime," a woman said with heartless cheer. "Don't you think we ought to turn him over and see if his front's affected?"

"Get your mind out of the gutter, Sophie. His front's just fine, and it's nothing you haven't seen before." More scrubbing along his backbone, the feel of it like raw coals being dug into his skin. He didn't even quiver, interested to hear how this conversation was going to continue.

"Oh, I don't know. He's pretty cute. Lab explosion, did you say? Does that mean he's going to turn into the Incredible Hulk every time he gets angry?" Sophie asked.

"Very funny. We're almost finished with him. Why don't you check his pupils while I see about getting him upstairs for observation?"

He felt her walk around him. Her hands were cool on his face. She started to pull open his eyelid, and he glared at her. "Get your rubber-gloved hands off me, woman," he snapped.

She jumped back with a startled shriek. She was just the kind of woman he usually found attractive—blond and pretty and stupid. He wondered how Suzanna Molloy was faring.

"You're awake," she said needlessly.

A white-coated doctor pushed Sophie out of the way, trying to look efficient, as if he hadn't been obsessed with football a few moments ago. "That dose of morphine must have worn off too quickly. Are you in much pain?"

"Not when you keep your hands off me," he snarled. "Where are my clothes?"

"Er—we had to cut them off you. Someone from Beebe Systems was going to see about getting you some new ones. You won't be needing them for a while. We're admitting you for observation."

"The hell you are."

"Dr. Crompton, you've been through quite an ordeal. We need to make sure you've suffered no head trauma, that the goop on your skin won't cause a reaction. We need—"

"I need my clothes. If someone doesn't provide me some within the next two hours, I'm walking out of this place naked."

The doctor looked at him warily, trying for a cheerful smile, only to have it fade again. "You're kidding."

"You can't keep me here against my will, and you know it as well as I do."

"It's my professional opinion—"

"I don't give squat about your professional opinion. Two hours." He lay back down again and closed his eyes. Damn them and their drugs! As if his body hadn't been through enough, he still had to fight off the effects of the narcotic they'd pumped through his system. "Get me Osborn," he said.

"I'm not sure if Mr. Osborn is still at the hospital."

"He's here," Daniel said grimly. "Tell him he's got five minutes."

He was there in less than three, and he didn't come alone. Daniel didn't bother to lift his head, but he knew that Osborn had at least two people in tow. Doubtless General Armstead, and either Jackson or maybe one of the Green Beret types that mysteriously wandered the halls at Beebe. He didn't care—he was too busy concentrating on the strange feelings that were sweeping over his body. Not unpleasant, they seemed to be seeping through his abraded back, sending little electrical charges through the surface of his skin.

"How are you doing, Dan?" Osborn's hearty voice boomed. "You gave us quite a scare."

Daniel considered his options for a brief, satisfying moment. One of those included throttling Osborn, a sorely tempting fantasy but one which, in the end, would avail him nothing. He'd never been a man who was prey to his emotions, and he wasn't about to become one now.

"What happened?" he asked in a deceptively neutral voice, opening his eyes. He'd been right. Retired General Jack Armstead stood a few feet away, his bulldog face creased into a look of concern, one that was belied by the alert, dangerous expression in his colorless eyes. The Green Beret type was a man named Cole Slaughter, and he didn't look any friendlier. Daniel wondered idly what happened to Jackson.

"One of your experiments must have gone awry," Osborn was saying. "Unlike you, of course, but you must have forgotten what you were doing. Jackson said he smelled something burning. If he hadn't alerted security, we might not have been able to get you out in time."

"Ah, yes, Jackson. A useful man," Daniel murmured, not bothering to deny Osborn's convenient theory. "Where is he?"

Daniel wasn't a sensitive man, but he was an observant one, and even in his current state he recognized the quick shift of communication between Armstead and Osborn. He filed it away for later examination.

"Slaughter drove him home," Armstead said. "He was pretty shaken up this afternoon after you attacked him."

Daniel didn't bother to deny it. "How is Ms. Molloy?"

"The woman who was with you? No one knew who she was—she didn't have any identification on her, apart from a Beebe tag, and that was phony. What'd you say her name was?"

"Suzanna Molloy."

Henry Osborn swore with more emotion than he'd shown since Daniel's lab had blown apart. "The reporter? What the hell was she doing there?"

"What's going on here, Osborn?" Armstead demanded. "Your security sucks. I'll have that woman arrested for trespassing."

"No, you won't." Daniel levered himself up to look at his three visitors. "She was there at my invitation." He wasn't quite sure why he lied—it merely seemed the next logical step.

"You invited her?" Osborn said. "But why? We don't want the press involved in our work. She's too nosy as it is. How do you know she didn't set the explosion?"

"Was it set?" Daniel asked pleasantly.

Osborn recovered quickly. "Damned if I know. Industrial sabotage isn't unheard of, and you're not the type to make careless mistakes."

"No," said Daniel. "I'm not."

"We'll have the security staff question her as soon as she regains consciousness," Armstead announced. "Slaughter, see to it. I want answers."

"You'll leave her alone," Daniel said evenly.

"Daniel, be reasonable," Osborn pleaded.

"I always am. Ms. Molloy is a friend of mine. An intimate friend of mine. She was there to spend time with me, and for no other reason." It was a flat-out lie, but for the time being his only defense against Osborn's trickiness was to lie, and sex was the one thing the man would find believable.

"Do you think it's wise to sleep with someone in her position?" Osborn asked with great disapproval.

"It depends which position she's in."

They didn't even crack a smile. "This isn't like you, Daniel," Osborn said.

Crompton considered it as the door swung silently shut behind the three men. No, it wasn't like him at all. And he was feeling oddly playful for a man who'd just survived a murder attempt.

He had no doubt whatsoever that that was what it had been. He wouldn't have left a volatile compound simmering if the pope had summoned him. He'd had his share of lab explosions in the past—what research scientist hadn't?—but what he was currently working on involved nothing more dangerous than potential eyestrain and carpal tunnel syndrome. He'd been glued to his computer for months now, checking and rechecking. The only work he'd done under the hood had been to keep the legion of spies off the scent.

He sat up gingerly, staring around him at the sterile examining room, flexing his sore muscles. Maybe it was something as elemental as surviving death that was making him feel so unnaturally energetic. The sense of well-being was thrumming through him. God, he almost felt like smiling.

First off, he needed to find Molloy, to see what kind of shape she was in. Now that he'd identified her, he didn't trust Armstead and his goons not to harass her. Besides, even though he'd taken the brunt of the explosion and the green slime, apparently she was still unconscious. He wanted to see what she felt like when she woke up. Would she have the same sense of well-being? The same tingling, burning sensation in her skin?

And he wanted to see if she still had the same inexplicable effect on him, a combination of fury and attraction. No one was going to stop him from finding out.

AT LEAST THE ROOM was relatively dark. Suzanna could hear the sounds of the hospital behind the curtained alcove, the quiet hush of rubber-soled shoes on polished vinyl floors, the hiss and thump of medical equipment, the muffled murmur of voices. She'd been awake for a while, alone in this anonymous room, but no one had come to check on her.

Just as well. She felt odd, disoriented, and she wanted time to herself, to consider what had happened to her.

She'd fainted, like some damned Victorian heroine. She'd collapsed gracefully in Daniel Crompton's arms, and it wouldn't have surprised her if he'd dropped her on the ground. The man was not equipped with the most advanced set of social graces.

But she didn't think he had. She could still remember him holding her, she could still feel that strange, wrenching sensation, when they'd taken her away from him. He hadn't wanted to let her go.

Now where did that absurd thought come from? If Crompton hadn't wanted to let her go, it was because he'd wanted to shake the truth out of her. Hadn't he practically accused her of sabotaging his lab? Brilliant the man might be, but when it came to common sense he seemed to be lacking. If she'd set him up, she wouldn't have waited around, arguing with him. She would have gotten the hell out of there.

Her hands were burning. She glanced down at them. They looked the same—strong, long-fingered, with no jewelry. She'd seen those hands all her life, and yet suddenly they looked different to her.

The door opened silently, and a shadowy form stepped into the dimly lit room. She recognized that shape, even before he stepped into the light, and she let out a sigh of relief.

"Uncle Vinnie," she whispered, holding out her hands to him.

He advanced into the room, a short, squat figure, no more than five feet three inches tall and almost as round, wearing a suit that probably cost more than the entire contents of Suzanna's closet. It didn't help. His thinning gray hair was pasted across his scalp, and his own rings made up for Suzanna's lack of jewelry.

"I blame myself," he said morosely, taking her hands in his.

"Don't be ridiculous, Uncle Vinnie," she protested, ignoring the pain his grip caused her. "You gave me a tip. I followed up on it. It just goes to show you were right—there is something funny going on at Beebe."

"You might have been killed," he protested, releasing one hand and heaving his bulk into a seat beside the bed.

Suzanna managed a wry smile. "Only the good die young."

"Don't be ridiculous, *cara*. You may be able to fool the others, but you've never been able to fool your Uncle Vinnie."

"You're not my Uncle Vinnie," she pointed out. "You're Francesca's Uncle Vinnie, and I've told you a hundred times I really don't need you to watch out for me."

Vinnie waved a plump hand, dismissing her protests. "You let me be the judge of that. A young girl like you, on your own in a man's world . . ."

"I'm not that young. Twenty-seven," she pointed out.

"You're young for your age. Now my Francesca, she marrried right out of that high-priced college the two of you attended, and she's got her husband and her husband's family to look out for her. I'm a lonely old man with too much time on my hands. I need someone to fuss over, you know that as well as I do."

"Uncle Vinnie," she said gently, "you are neither old, nor lonely, and you certainly don't have too much time on your hands. I don't understand why you persist in thinking I need watching over."

"I promised Francesca. Besides, since I've retired, I need something to keep me busy."

"You haven't retired, Uncle Vinnie," Suzanna said.

"I haven't been down to the restaurant in more than a month," he protested.

"You may have retired from the restaurant business, but you haven't retired from your career. Let's face it, Uncle Vinnie, you're a crook."

"I'm a businessman," he corrected, not the slightest bit offended. "My friends and I, we have investments—"

"Rackets," Suzanna supplied.

"And we look after our own."

"I'm not your own, Uncle Vinnie."

"Once you became Francesca's best friend and college roommate, you became family. And nothing's going to change that. You won't let me help you, but at least you'll let me warn you. And what do you do? Instead of keeping away from danger, you walk right into it with open arms."

Suzanna managed a tired grin. "I'm hopeless."

"I don't like what's going on at Beebe, Suzanna. Even with my connections, I can't find who's behind the organization, but it doesn't look good. You need to keep away from them."

"At least I don't need to worry about BBCSI being run by organized crime," she said.

"Very funny," he said stiffly. "There are worse things than our little fraternal organization. You're out of your league, there, Suzanna. Leave it to the experts."

"I don't even know what it is I'd be leaving."

"It's big," Vinnie said.

"I imagine so, considering the way people are reacting. Someone tried to kill Dr. Crompton today."

Vinnie's pouchy eyes narrowed. "You're sure of that?"

"Reasonably sure. They almost sent me with him."

Uncle Vinnie muttered something in Italian he assumed Suzanna was too innocent to understand. Fortunately Francesca had taught her every dirty word she knew, and the force of that expletive did more to convince Suzanna how desperate things were than anything since the lab had first exploded. "So it's gone that far already," he muttered, half to himself. "And now everyone knows it."

"Everyone knows what?"

"That whatever he was working on, he's succeeded. No one would risk that man's life if he hadn't come up with something worth vastly more. You know what his reputation is, don't you? America's secret weapon? And if they're ready to sacrifice him, rather than let him cause trouble, then he must have come up with an even more effective weapon."

"Weapon?" Suzanna echoed, shocked. "You think he was working on some kind of weapon?"

"Everything nowadays can be used as a weapon. If he was working for the good of mankind, do you think someone would have tried to blow up his lab, with him in it? No, Suzanna," he said sadly. "What about a little trip? Have you ever been to Venice?"

"I'm not going anywhere."

"It's not just up to me. I'll protect you if I can, but even I have bosses. People to answer to, and they're all far too interested in what's going on at Beebe. I can't be sure I can keep you safe. The stakes are too high."

"And exactly what are the stakes?"

Uncle Vinnie shook his head slowly. "I don't even want to guess. My people will look out for you, *cara*. To the best of their ability. But if you have any sense at all, you'll stay as far away from Dr. Crompton as you can. The man's living on borrowed time. Whatever he's discovered has already fallen into the wrong hands, and he's too knowledgeable, too dangerous, to let live."

"Wouldn't that be killing the goose that laid the golden egg?" she argued.

"Not when they've got the formula for making those golden eggs. Who needs a goose that you have to feed and take care of?" Uncle Vinnie said philosophically. "What about Paris?"

"I'm not going anywhere."

Uncle Vinnie just looked at her. "I'll put the word out. No one will touch you. But you keep away from Dr. Crompton. I don't want any accidents. If and when he gets his, I don't want you within range. Do you understand?"

"Vinnie..."

But he'd already moved toward the door, silent despite his bulk. "Watch your back, *cara*. And keep away from that man."

He was gone before she could utter another protest, and she leaned back against the pillow, letting out her pent-up breath. Ever since Uncle Vinnie had come into her life almost ten years ago, he'd been mysterious and beneficent, a wise, almost comical figure, there when she needed a shoulder to cry on, an ear to listen to her problems. It had taken all her determination to keep him from pulling strings for her. If it had been up to Vinnie, she'd

probably be managing editor at the *Washington Post* by
this time.

But she'd made it brutally clear that what she had in
this life she intended to earn. She'd had too easy a life.
She was the only child of doting parents with too much
money. When they'd died while she was still in college,
all Uncle Vinnie's protective instincts had come into play,
but Suzanna needed to fend for herself. After twenty
years of having things handed to her, she was suddenly
out on her own, and she'd been determined to make her
own way, without Vinnie pulling strings. She'd accepted
his friendship, and even the occasional tip, but she wasn't
about to let him tender any offers on her behalf that
people couldn't refuse.

Keep away from Dr. Crompton, he'd said, and she'd
be wise to listen when a man like Uncle Vinnie spoke. If
Vinnie said Crompton was a doomed man, then it was
highly unlikely Suzanna could do anything to save him,
and she wasn't quite sure she wanted to. The man was
overbearing, unpleasant and too damned smart for his
own good. He was just the kind of man she found most
irritating, and she preferred thinking of him as the enemy.

Unfortunately, it wasn't going to be that clear-cut.
Somebody else saw Daniel Crompton as the enemy,
someone who used noxious fumes and sneak attacks and
who didn't care if someone besides Crompton got killed,
as well.

Suzanna had the choice of siding with Crompton or
siding with the forces of darkness, which meant she
didn't really have much choice at all.

Of course, Vinnie had meant for her to steer clear of
the whole thing. But she couldn't. Not with an organiza-

tion like Beebe Control Systems International in her back-yard, one shrouded in secrecy and security worthy of national defense. Crompton might work for them, but she wouldn't put it past them to be behind that lab explosion.

Maybe it wasn't a murder attempt. Maybe it was just a warning. But a warning against what? And how in heaven's name was she going to find out exactly what he was working on?

The lab was trashed now. She hadn't found anything of interest in the few minutes she'd had before Crompton's precipitous return, but she suspected he didn't keep his most important work there. Whoever bombed the place wouldn't have dared risk destroying it.

His home was the obvious place to check. She needed to get out of this hospital and go check out the place. He had to be in worse shape than she was—he'd been covered with that revolting green slime that had burned her hands. He'd be in the hospital for days, but if she didn't get moving soon, someone would get to his home before she did.

She swung her legs over the side of the bed. She was wearing one of those damnable hospital nightgowns. It was slit up the back and chilling her spine, and the bath-robe looked as if it were made out of ancient dish towels. Nothing, however, compared with the foam-rubber slippers. Suzanna wondered whether she could fashion a sari out of the sheet.

She wasn't alone. There'd been no sound, not even a whisper of noise, but the air around her shifted, and she looked up, staring at the tall figure in the doorway.

Another damned doctor, she thought wearily. This one in hospital greens, as if he'd just come from the operating room, or was about to return to it.

"Go away," she said flatly. "I've been poked and prodded enough. You're not doing any more tests."

He moved forward, into the pool of light, and she had an unpleasant shock as she looked up into Daniel Crompton's dark, cool eyes. She realized that those eyes were traveling up her long, bare legs with far too much leisurely interest. And that the feel of his eyes on her skin burned almost as much as the green slime had.

"What are you doing here?" she demanded, wishing her voice didn't sound slightly husky.

"They said you were unconscious."

"I'm not."

"No, more's the pity. Are you always this pleasant?"

"About the same as you," she replied tartly.

He ignored her taunt, moving across the room so silently it took her a moment to realize his feet were bare. The sight of his long, narrow feet was so startling that she didn't realize he'd picked up her hand in his and was busy taking her pulse. He began tapping her wrist.

She tried to yank away, but his fingers tightened. "I just want to test your reflexes," he said in an irritated voice.

"'Trust me, I'm a doctor'?" she murmured. "My reflexes have been checked plenty, and they're just fine, thank you. How are yours?"

"Fast."

"Jolly."

"Too fast," he said enigmatically, still holding her hand. She only wished she didn't find an odd sort of comfort in it. "How do you feel?"

"Like a wall fell on me."

"That was me."

She felt a moment's compunction. "I didn't thank you for saving my life."

He shrugged. "I'm not sure I did. Have you had any visitors?"

Suzanna thought of Uncle Vinnie and was glad she never blushed when she lied. "No. Were you expecting anyone?"

"If a man named Osborn tries to talk to you, refuse to see him. The same goes for Armstead, and just about anyone else."

Curiouser and curiouser, Suzanna thought, staring up at the man. "Isn't Osborn your boss? The president of Beebe?"

"He wants to know what you were doing in my lab at the time of the explosion. He doesn't trust you, Ms. Molloy. He thinks you might have rigged the explosion."

"And what do you think, Dr. Crompton?"

He reached out and put his hand along the side of her neck, his fingers long and cool and deft against her heated skin. "I think your pulse is racing, Ms. Molloy. I think you need a good long rest, with no visitors."

It was no wonder her pulse was racing, she thought irritably. Daniel Crompton was a vastly irritating man—he was enough to stir anybody's blood.

"What about you?" she asked abruptly.

"I'm getting out of here. But if I were you, Molloy, I'd stay put. At least here you're relatively safe."

"Why wouldn't I be safe?"

He shrugged, an abrupt, oddly appealing gesture. "I don't know. But it might be wiser not to ask anyone."

A moment later he was gone, and she was alone once more in her hospital room, using the very curses Uncle Vinnie had as she stared at the closed door in frustration.

...

Chapter Three

Daniel wondered why his feet weren't cold. He tended to
be oblivious to physical discomfort, but right now he was
intensely aware of every minuscule reaction his body was
going through, and walking barefoot down a sidewalk at
half past five o'clock on a late spring morning in northern California should have been downright chilly. Particularly since he was wearing nothing but the loose green
scrub suit he'd stolen from a locker at the hospital.

It wasn't particularly warm outside—he knew that. His
instincts told him it was hovering around fifty, and yet he
felt entirely comfortable, almost hot. His skin no longer
burned, but it tingled, pleasantly enough, and he felt an
odd tickle between his eyes.

His arms were hanging loosely by his sides as he moved
along, and he contented himself with twitching his nose
a couple of times as he stared absently at an old VW bug
parked on a side street.

The VW burst into flames.

The fireball of heat threw him back against a building, and he stayed there, dazed, uncomprehending. It
usually took a great deal to surprise him, but the explosion left him in a state of shock, and it took him a mo-

ment or two to steady himself, glance around to see whether someone had lobbed a grenade, or a mortar, or whatever it was people used to blow up things.

The streets were deserted. Lights were coming on in the buildings surrounding him, but there was no sign of anyone around. In the distance he could hear the faint wail of a fire alarm, and decided it was time to make himself scarce.

He ducked down a back alleyway, disappearing into the night. He wasn't in the mood to listen to questions, particularly when he hadn't the faintest idea what the answers were. While he'd never been one to let the stresses of ordinary living get to him, the last twenty-four hours had been enough to rattle the most phlegmatic of men. He'd had his lab invaded, he'd been sabotaged, poked, prodded, and now it seemed as if someone had set off a bomb just as he was walking by, and he could hardly count that a coincidence. To top it all off, he felt strange, restless, edgy and in a towering bad mood.

He moved through the early-morning light swiftly, away from the devastation of the burning automobile, trying to shake the sense of uneasiness that was plaguing him. He lived as anonymously as possible, in a box of a condominium in a box of a building, and by the time he neared his neighborhood he was running, at the comfortable loping jog he'd perfected. It was getting lighter by the minute, it was now close to 6:00 a.m., and he wondered whether the hospital or Beebe had anyone out looking for him.

The enclave of bland, architecturally atrocious buildings came equipped with a security guard and gate, something he'd never thought much about in the past. In his current position, he wasn't in the mood to talk to anyone, answer questions or even have to put up with someone looking at him strangely. All he wanted was to get back to his apartment, lock the door behind him, lie down on his futon and clear his mind. Until he could come up with a reason why someone would want to kill him.

He decided to wait until six, hoping against hope that the guard's shift might end, and he could slip through when he wasn't looking. He still had his watch, a fact which surprised him, and he stared at it, willing it to move to six.

When it did, he almost wished it hadn't. The prickling sensation that had been nagging at him suddenly washed over his body full force, and a blinding pain shot through his head, so fierce he thought of the VW and wondered whether his own brain was going to explode. His stomach cramped, and he sank to his knees on the pavement, no longer caring that the guard was going to see him. The man would probably call the police, or at least an ambulance, and Crompton would be back where he started, his escape for nothing.

Slowly, slowly, the pain began to abate. The rush that spread over his body settled into an edgy kind of heat, and he managed to lift his head, expecting to meet the security guard's curious gaze. Or perhaps even his gun.

The security guard was standing in his little box, guarding the gate. He was smoking a cigarette, glancing idly in the direction of Daniel's hunched-over figure with all the interest of a toad.

Daniel staggered to his feet, both relieved and incensed. Not that he wanted the man to pay attention to him, but he might at least have shown some concern for the security of the building. Not to mention the welfare of one of its tenants.

He advanced on the man, angry enough to brazen it out, only to come up short. The security guard had his name, which was Doyle, emblazoned across his pocket. And Doyle was looking straight through him as if he wasn't even there.

The hell with him, Crompton thought, circling the security gate and striding past the oblivious guard, fully determined to ignore any belated questions or calls to stop.

There was no abrupt shout or even a tentative question as Daniel reached the door of his anonymous building. The guard didn't seem to realize he existed.

It wasn't until that moment that Daniel realized his keys were somewhere back at the hospital, along with his slime-splattered clothes, his wallet and his shoes. "Hell and damnation," he muttered, wheeling around, prepared to go to the oblivious Doyle and demand that he open the door for him.

Doyle was no longer oblivious. He looked like a bloodhound who'd scented a juicy pheasant on the wind. Alert, head cocked, listening, he stared just over Daniel's head.

Was the man blind, or drunk, or just abysmally stupid? Daniel neither knew nor cared, he simply wanted to get up to his apartment, get out of his stolen scrub suit and take a shower, to wash the hot, prickling feeling from his skin.

The door opened, and an early-morning jogger stepped out into the cool air. Daniel grabbed the door before it could swing shut again, muttered a terse thanks and disappeared into the building.

His fourth-floor apartment was an easier matter, since he was smart enough to leave a key under a loose section of the carpeting in the hallway. Within moments he was safe inside, the door locked behind him.

He was oddly breathless, shaken, and his brain was awash with a thousand anomalies, too many things that made no sense, particularly to his own orderly mind. The way that car had burst into flames. The guard's oblivion. The brief flash of shock on the jogger's face when Daniel had brushed past him.

Not to mention the odd, fuzzy look of his hand as he'd opened his front door.

He stared down at his body and knew something had to be wrong with his vision. He looked foggy and slightly out of focus but when he raised his head, the apartment was clear and precise. It was only his body that seemed blurred.

He rubbed a hand across his eyes, but it didn't help. The morning light was filling the ascetic confines of his apartment, but he didn't bother closing the curtains. They might be looking for him, and his home was the logical place to try to find him. Since Doyle and the jogger had been too sleepy or hung over to notice his return, he might be able to remain in hiding for at least the few hours he needed for a shower and a nap.

The hot water spat like tiny needles onto his skin, but he was inured to the discomfort. He stood in the shower for what seemed like hours, trying to wash away that odd, heated sensitivity that covered him, but it was useless. Turning off the water, he stepped out into his steamed-up bathroom, grabbing a towel and wrapping it around his damp body. Maybe a shave would wake him up.

His bathroom mirror was completely fogged. He reached out and rubbed the condensation from its surface. And then he rubbed again.

There was no reflection whatsoever in the mirror, not even the towel that was wrapped around his torso.

There'd been a phrase he'd read long ago, in some melodramatic novel. Something about one's blood running cold. Suddenly he knew exactly what that phrase meant.

He slammed open the bathroom door, heading for the bedroom and the mirror over his dresser.

Nothing. He could see the plain, white-covered bed behind him, the unadorned white walls, the pile of books on the nightstand. But he couldn't see his own, slightly out of focus, shower-damp body at all.

"Oh, no," he murmured, utterly fascinated. "I'm invisible."

SUZANNA CONSIDERED following him. Daniel Crompton had simply disappeared from her hospital room like a wraith, and if she'd had just the slightest bit more energy, not to mention a slightly more modest outfit, she would have climbed out of that hospital bed and gone after him.

As it was, her feet barely touched the floor before she sank back, groaning. Her head throbbed, her skin tingled, and her temper was not the sweetest.

Nor was it improved by the sound of voices breaking the early-morning hush of the hospital corridors.

"I'm afraid I must insist, nurse," the man said. "There's been a serious breach of security at Beebe, and a question of sabotage. If you won't let me question Ms.

Molloy then I'm afraid I'm going to have to take action."

"You can question her all you want," came the tart reply, "during visiting hours, and if her doctor gives permission and she's willing. Until then, Mr. Osborn, you'd better leave."

There was a moment of silence. And the unmistakable sound of crinkling paper that was undoubtedly green. "Five minutes," the nurse said, her shoes squeaking as she made her retreat.

By the time the door opened, Suzanna was lying in perfect stillness, her eyes shut, her breathing shallow, not a flicker betraying her awareness. She would have liked to steal just a tiny glance at this Mr. Osborn who was so determined to get his own way. He was one of the people Crompton had warned her about. An odd thought, an SOB like Crompton looking out for her. It could almost make her smile.

"Are you awake, Ms. Molloy?"

Suzanna didn't move.

"They told me you'd regained consciousness several hours ago, and no one mentioned giving you any additional drugs to help you sleep. Open your eyes, Ms. Molloy. I have no intention of leaving until I talk with you."

Suzanna managed a faint, very believable snore.

To her dismay she heard Osborn seat himself in the plastic chair beside her hospital bed. "If you prefer, we'll play it that way," he said. "Allow me to introduce myself. I'm Henry Osborn, CEO of Beebe Control Systems. I imagine a clever girl like you already knew that. What you might not know is that I can be a very dangerous man to cross, or a very helpful man, if I'm feeling generous. You've been a boil on our behind for the last six months with your incessant questions, but we've been forbearing, believing in the right of a free press."

Osborn was the kind of man who believed in total control of the press, but Suzanna managed to keep from voicing that opinion.

"I want to know what you saw in Dr. Crompton's lab before the unfortunate accident. Your help in this matter could be invaluable, and we're known to reward those who help us."

It was no accident, Suzanna thought, and you know it. She let out another gentle little snore, wondering whether she was overdoing it.

"On the other hand," Osborn continued smoothly, ignoring her act, "you were trespassing on private property. You had a phony ID tag, and we haven't ruled out the possibility of industrial sabotage. We could push it as far as attempted murder, Ms. Molloy, and you're our obvious suspect. I don't believe what Crompton told me about you for one moment."

He was good, Suzanna had to admit it. She was dying to know what Crompton had told him. It took all her formidable willpower to keep from reacting.

He rose, and she could feel him move toward her. "We'll be watching you, Ms. Molloy," he said softly. "If we can't get to you here, we'll wait till you leave. Sooner or later you're going to tell us what you know. What you saw." And she felt his hand on her breast, squeezing it painfully thruogh the layers of hospital cotton.

She couldn't control her start of pain, but she played it through, opening her eyes for a deliberately dazed moment, then shuttering them again, uttering no more than a plaintive moan before she ostensibly drifted off again.

"I could almost believe you, Ms. Molloy," the nasty little sadist murmured. "If I were just a little more gullible. I'll be back."

Suzanna almost snorted. She couldn't imagine anyone less like the Terminator than the brief glimpse she'd had of elegant, white-haired Henry Osborn. Except that he might be just as merciless.

The door closed with a sigh, but Suzanna didn't move. She held still, waiting until she was certain he was truly gone. Uncle Vinnie had been right, but then, she'd never had cause to doubt him in the first place. There was something extremely nasty going on at Beebe Control Systems, and while sabotage doubtless had something to do with it, she put her money on the deceptively charming gentleman who'd just mauled her breast. If only she knew what Crompton had told him!

Doubtless nothing flattering. But it hadn't been the truth, either, or Osborn wouldn't have hesitated in having her arrested for suspected sabotage, as he'd threatened to do. Obviously Osborn had his secrets, and he wanted to know exactly which ones of those Suzanna had been privy to.

She let her eyes drift open, still keeping her breathing regulated. The room was empty, the early-morning light sending strange shadows against the pale green walls. It was just after six, and in the far distance she could hear the wailing sounds of a fire siren.

She sat up, moving quietly, and slid from the bed. One thing was certain: she wasn't going to stay there and wait until Osborn could summon his goons to watch over her. Assuming he had goons to summon. She needed to get out of this place, and she needed to find out what was really going on with Daniel Crompton. She'd almost been killed, just because she was in the wrong place at the wrong time, and her breast still throbbed from Osborn's nasty grope. She wanted to know what Crompton had told him, she wanted to know what the man was working on, and she wanted to know whether either of them was still in danger.

And there was only one way to find out.

She had to ask him. No, scratch that—she had to sit the man down and force him to tell her what was going on. Exactly how she planned to do that was still a mystery, but she'd always relied on her ability to improvise when things got a little complicated. First things first.

At least they'd brought her clothes back, a little the worse for wear, her ratty running shoes still usable. The great Dr. Daniel Crompton might have no qualms about going out barefoot in stolen hospital garb, but Suzanna was a little more discreet.

Her borrowed lab coat had taken the brunt of the slime assault. Suzanna dressed quickly, grateful that apart from the tingling in her hands and an odd heat at the back of her eyes, she seemed to be in fairly good shape. As a matter of fact, the worst of her discomfort still came from where Osborn had mauled her. Interesting.

The corridors were coming to life as she stepped out of her room, but she'd already learned that the best way to get away with something was to look as if you knew what you were doing. She strode down the hallway quite purposefully, not dodging when she passed an orderly's curious gaze, and a moment later ducked down a deserted stairwell. She was free.

If she'd had any sense at all, she would have headed straight home, barricaded herself inside her second-floor apartment, put something cool and jazzy on the stereo and gone to sleep.

But she didn't feel particularly sensible. The old Victorian house she lived in was more than a mile away, on the far side of town, her car was presumably still at Beebe, and she knew for a fact that Dr. Daniel Crompton's apartment was much closer—only a brief walk away.

He might not be there, of course. But if she'd gotten into a place with security as tight as BBCSI, then she had little doubt she could get into his apartment. There was no way she was going to rest until she got some answers.

DANIEL WAS ENJOYING himself immensely, not in the slightest bit disturbed about his new body. He could feel himself, see himself, albeit slightly out of focus. If he dropped the towel on a surface in front of the mirror he could see that, as well. If he picked it up again it seemed to float in midair. If he draped it around him, it disappeared.

It made no earthly sense, in terms of physics or any known science. He tried it with various other items. Any piece of clothing he held would still be corporeal, but once he put it on it vanished. He wandered through his apartment, wearing only a pair of old jeans that he usually preferred not to be seen in. At least this time he wouldn't have to worry, he thought with dark humor.

Once he put food in his mouth, it disappeared, and he swallowed half a quart of his special multivitamin energy drink that usually sufficed instead of regular food, washing it down with at least a gallon of coffee. He turned on the news, something he seldom bothered wtih, but the brief story about the explosion at Beebe was the company line. He stared at Henry Osborn's cool, concerned face and muttered an expletive.

Which reminded him. If people couldn't see him, and that doubtless explained why the guard and the jogger seemed to be ignoring him, would they be able to hear him?

All in the nature of scientific experiment, he dialed Henry Osborn's unlisted number. His ruthlessly elegant, ruthlessly slim wife, Doris, answered the phone. He'd never liked her, either the insufferably smug way she moved through the few social functions he'd been forced to attend, or the way she'd delicately, unmistakably come on to him on one of those same occasions, letting her slender, bejeweled hand rest high up on his thigh. She was a barracuda, well-suited to her husband.

He started with a little heavy breathing.

"Is anyone there?" Doris demanded, cool and imperious as ever.

He kept his voice low, husky, unrecognizable, as he murmured a couple of graphic suggestions he would have been far more interested in trying with Ms. Suzanna Molloy.

There was a shocked intake of breath on the other end, leaving him in no doubt that even if people couldn't see him, they could certainly hear him. And then elegant Doris Osborn said, "I told you not to call me here, Dorfio. We'll meet at the health club, as always." Before Daniel had time to recover from his shock, she'd hung up the phone.

Dismissing her with a reluctant laugh, he went about his experiments. If he was invisible, perhaps he had other gifts, as well. One thing was certain—he hadn't been invisible in the hospital. Suzanna Molloy had looked up at him out of those distrustful brown eyes, and there'd been no mistaking the hostility in them. Nor the reluctant fascination. While Daniel didn't usually waste time paying attention to how people responded to him, in Suzanna's case he didn't consider it a waste. For some reason he had yet to fathom, she fascinated him. It only made sense that he'd be interested in her reaction.

He must have been visible as he walked through the town. That car exploding couldn't have been an accident, not after the events of the day. Someone must have been waiting for him, armed with some kind of heavy artillery.

But by the time he'd reached his apartment building, he'd been gone. He could remember that strange, tingling feeling, like a hot flash, that had spread over him just as it neared 6:00 a.m., and he could only guess that that was when it had started. The question was, how long was it going to last?

He flicked off the television, then held very still. Someone was outside the door. Knocking, with a fair amount of insistence. He wasn't in the mood for visitors, or for answering the door. It would only be someone from Beebe, trying to harass him again.

If it was someone from work, it was someone who had few qualms about breaking and entering. Whoever stood outside his door was fiddling with his lock.

He glanced around him, considering where to hide, and then realized he had no need to. He could stand right there, motionless, soundless, and whoever was attempting to break into his apartment wouldn't even know he was there.

He hadn't set the security lock when he'd first come in, a major oversight. He waited patiently as the lock finally gave and the door opened. There were any number of people who'd made a recent habit of breaking and entering his personal space, but he could only hope it was the one person he was interested in seeing at that particular moment.

It was. "Dr. Crompton?" Suzanna Molloy's faintly husky voice heralded her entrance. "Are you there?"

She knew damned well he wasn't, having knocked loudly. He watched as she stepped inside, closing the door quietly behind her, her brown eyes sweeping over the living room of his apartment, looking right through him.

"Typical," she muttered in disgust, stifling a yawn. She moved through the living room, glancing at the plain white walls, the piles of professional magazines, the lack of anything like a stereo or even a rug on the floor. Even his old small TV was probably black and white, a rarity in this modern age.

"He must be some kind of monk," she muttered, glancing at the narrow futon he occasionally slept on.

Not exactly, he thought, surveying the long sweep of her legs and the firm, gently rounded bottom beneath her faded jeans. She wasn't his type. But maybe he was ready to change his type.

It happened so fast he had no warning. She turned around, heading into the kitchen, and barreled, unseeing, right into him.

She fell backward, onto that luscious bottom he'd just been admiring, staring up in shock, staring at nothing. This could have its advantages, he thought, wondering whether he dared to so far as to touch her.

She shook her head, as if clearing cobwebs from her brain, and struggled back to her feet. "Keep your shirt on, Nancy Drew,'' she muttered out loud. He controlled the urge to offer her a hand. She wouldn't see it, and if she felt it, she'd probably scream.

He managed to avoid her as she moved tentatively into the little kitchen area he seldom used. He heard her open the refrigerator, then her remarkably graphic curse as she discovered just how empty it was.

"I'm starving," she moaned to herself. "And all the man seems to eat is moldy cheese and beer.''

He didn't bother correcting her. He moved back against the wall silently, so she wouldn't run into him again. The small electronic clock signaled it was now eight in the morning.

He felt that same, strange flush sweep over his body, and he leaned against the wall, trying to control the sudden weakness in his knees as the pain shot through him. He was shivering, praying for the moment to pass, when through the fog of pain he heard her strangled scream.

"How did you gèt in here?" she demanded, her voice filled with horror. And he opened his eyes to realize that for the first time in hours, someone was staring directly at him.

Chapter Four

For a moment Suzanna couldn't move. He stood only a few feet away from her, in the middle of his soulless living room, dressed in a faded pair of jeans that clung to his narrow hips and long legs. He wasn't wearing a shirt, despite the coolness of the morning air, and Suzanna decided then and there that a scientist shouldn't have such a chest. He should have been pale and soft and flabby. Not toned and tanned and subtly well-muscled.

He hadn't bothered to tie back his hair, and it hung around his strong-featured face, making him look like a pirate, not a biochemist with a Ph.D. in physics on the side.

She managed, just barely, to pull herself together. "Where did you come from?"

"I live here, remember?" he replied in an even voice. "You're the one who's not supposed to be here. Where did you learn to pick locks?"

She could feel just a faint trace of color heat her cheeks, but she simply tilted her chin with a defiance she didn't completely feel. "I do what needs to be done."

"Including going to jail? Breaking and entering is a crime, last I heard, and you've done it twice in the last twenty-four hours. Were you planning on planting a bomb here, as well?" He asked the question with cool disdain, wandering past her shocked figure to stare out the window, giving her a full, distracting view of his back. It was almost sexier than his chest.

"Being able to pick a lock has nothing to do with being able to set a bomb," she said, tearing her gaze away reluctantly. "Why should I want to blow up your lab? Or your apartment, for that matter? I'm a reporter, not an industrial spy."

He glanced back at her over his shoulder. "It makes a good story."

"I'm not that desperate for a byline. You don't believe it, either," she added with sudden assurance. "What did you tell Osborn about me?"

Daniel turned and leaned against the wall, seemingly at ease in his partially dressed state. If only he'd just pull a shirt on over all that gorgeous flesh, she might be able to concentrate a little better. "So Osborn came to see you? I thought he would. What did he want to know?"

"What I saw in your lab."

"And what did you see in my lab?"

"You," she said.

"Is that what you told him?"

"I pretended to be asleep." She remembered the brutal feel of his hand on her, and she couldn't control a slight shiver of distaste.

"What did he do to you?" Crompton asked suddenly.

"What makes you think he did anything?" she countered, acutely uncomfortable.

"The expression on your face."

"You don't miss much, do you?"

"I'm a scientist. I'm trained to observe. Did he hurt you?"

For some reason she didn't want to tell him. Tell him that the CEO of a multinational corporation groped her breast, that an elegant, middle-aged businessman hurt her. It was both embarrassing and unbelievable. "Do you think he's the kind of man who would?" she said instead.

He stared at her for a long moment. He had really wonderful eyes, she realized, but then, that was in keeping with the rest of him. They were a dark, mesmerizing blue, almost black, and yet she could almost imagine tiny pinpricks of golden light, almost like flames, at their center. Scientists were supposed to be nerds. How come she got trapped with the one gorgeous one?

"I wouldn't have thought so," Crompton said, dropping down on the uncomfortable-looking futon. "But you're acting like he molested you."

"Hardly," she said in her driest voice. "And you still haven't told me what you said about me. Whatever it was, he didn't believe it."

"You had quite a conversation, considering you were pretending to be unconscious," he observed.

"He was doing all the talking."

Daniel considered her for a moment, and she wished there was some place she didn't mind looking. His chest was too distracting, his eyes, his mouth, his hands were far too strong and elegant. She concentrated on his left shoulder, trying to ignore the bone and muscle. She'd always had a weakness for slightly bony shoulders, and Daniel Crompton's were just about perfect.

"I told him you were visiting me," he said after a long moment, stretching his legs out in front of him. "I didn't want him to jump to any conclusions if he heard you'd broken in."

"Why not?"

"He'd be more than happy to concentrate his energies on prosecuting you, when I know perfectly well you didn't set any kind of incendiary device in my lab. Whoever did it would get away scot-free, while you languished in jail."

She pushed her hair away from her face in what she hoped was a suitably no-nonsense gesture. "I never languish."

The smile was small, only a faint quirk at the corner of his mouth. It nevertheless managed to transform his entire face, from the austere, elegant beauty to something infinitely more approachable. "I imagine you don't," he drawled.

Suzanna didn't want to approach him. "You think it was set?"

"I see that journalist's mind of yours clicking away. If I had any sense I'd kick you and your questions out of here."

"I haven't quite figured out why you haven't," she admitted.

He surveyed her with a clinical air, and it took all her self-control not to glance down at her own appearance. She knew perfectly well what she looked like, and she'd never been one for spending needless time fussing with her reflection in a mirror. She had bluntly cut, dirty-blond hair, though her mother referred to it as wheat-colored, which certainly sounded a lot more attractive. Her nose was unimpressive, her brown eyes large but disguised by the wire-rimmed glasses she wore. She seemed taller than average, her figure the typically ten-pounds-overweight American female figure, and she wore an exclusive uniform of baggy jeans and rude T-shirts. The current one was a faded fuchsia with the logo Eat Quiche and Die emblazoned across it. She had never been the type to incite men's passions, and she doubted the estimable Dr. Daniel Crompton even possessed such passions. Even if, looking at him stretched shirtless across his futon, she wished he did.

"Neither have I," he said, shattering any irrational hope she might have had that he harbored a secret passion for her. "Maybe I'm putting up with you for the same reason people say they climb mountains."

No woman liked to hear herself mentioned in the same sentence as a mountain, but Suzanna swallowed her retort. "And why do people climb mountains?"

"Because they're there."

Not the greatest show of confidence, but she decided to take what she could get, before Crompton decided not to trust her. "All right," she said, glancing around the barren living room for a seat. There weren't any, just the futon, which was too small for the two of them. She compromised by sitting on the floor, wincing slightly as she sank down on the bare wood.

"Are you all right?"

He didn't miss a thing. She'd have to be extra careful around this man, for more reasons than one. "Just a little stiff from yesterday. I'm not used to being tossed on a floor and jumped on."

Again that faint glint of humor in his dark eyes. "It has its advantages."

She wasn't going to let him wow her. "Not if you're the one on the bottom," she shot back.

He shrugged, moving those gorgeous, bony shoulders of his, and she wondered what he'd say if she asked him to put on a shirt. Maybe he could even slick that long mane of hair back, find himself some ballpoint pens and a pocket protector. Hitch his jeans halfway up to his armpits, or better yet, find something polyester to wear.

It would be a major mistake to let him guess what kind of effect he was having on her. She tossed her hair back, meeting his gaze defiantly. "Who do you think sabotaged your lab?" she said. "And do you think they meant to hurt you, as well?"

"I never said I thought my lab was sabotaged."

"Give me a break, Crompton," she snapped. "You aren't the only person around here with a brain, even if yours is as oversized as your ego."

"All right. For argument's sake let's say someone set a bomb in my lab. You're the obvious suspect, but for now we're going to assume you had nothing to do with it. You simply happened to be in the wrong place at the wrong time."

"That's a matter of opinion," she said. "It's going to make great copy."

"I'm sure it will. When I let you write it."

"*Let* me write it?" she echoed, incensed. "I'd like to see you try to stop me, buster. There is such a thing as free speech, and a free press, and—"

"And if you want me to cooperate and tell you everything I know, then you'll have to cooperate with me," he interrupted smoothly. "I don't want anything going public until I'm sure it's safe."

"And you get to decide?"

"Take it or leave it."

He was maddening. He also held all the cards, and Suzanna knew it. Much as she wanted to tell him off, throw his conditions back in that too-handsome face, she had too much sense. The truth about what was going on at Beebe, rife as it was with industrial sabotage, would give her career the kind of boost most people only fantasized about. Add to that what Uncle Vinnie had referred to as America's secret weapon, and she had a story that would push her to the top of her profession.

"I'll take it," she said firmly. "On one condition."

"What's that?"

"You keep me with you. You can call me your research assistant, your significant other, your sister or your housekeeper. I don't care. You just make sure I'm in on things."

"My research assistants are working on their Ph.D.'s."

"I already have mine. Stanford, 1988, in physics," she said succinctly, hoping he'd be impressed.

He wasn't. "I don't have a sister, and I don't need a housekeeper."

She glanced around the pristine confines of his apartment with transparent contempt. "You certainly don't."

"So I suppose that makes you my mistress."

She blushed. It was the curse of her pale, freckled complexion, an inheritance from her Danish mother. "No," she said flatly.

"Think I'm going to take advantage, Molloy?" he said. "Use it as an excuse to grope you?"

She remembered Henry Osborn, and she shivered. "I know scientists," she said. "You spend so much time in the lab your hormones go awry, and it wouldn't matter if I looked like a truck driver in drag. How about your cousin from out of town?"

He shook his head. "Santa Cristina is a small town, Molloy. You're too well-known. If you won't pose as my mistress, how about a date? We can still be in the courting stage, not the falling-all-over-each-other stage."

"You *have* been locked in your lab too long," she observed coolly. "Mistresses, courting. You must have read historical romances in your childhood."

Again that small, devastating smile. "I've read my share."

She didn't believe him for a moment. "In this day and age, courtship, if it exists at all, consists of sharing lab tests before people do the deed," she said primly.

"Had a lot of experience, have you?"

"More than you've had," she shot back, ignoring the fact that she hadn't gone to bed with anyone since her short-lived, very unsatisfactory engagement three years earlier.

"You want to compare conquests?"

"You're not adding me to your list," she warned him.

"I wasn't aware that I was asking."

She wanted to hit him. "Just in case you were considering it," she said stonily.

"I'm forewarned," he said, still with that annoying trace of amusement. "Okay, so we're not supposed to be lovers. How about friends?"

She could be just as cynical. "That might be even harder to believe."

She startled him into laughing out loud. "Why don't we let them draw their own conclusions?"

"What if someone asks?"

"I'm entirely capable of refusing to answer rude questions. I imagine you could do so, as well. You don't strike me as the most cooperative person I've ever met." He rose from the futon, his movements smooth and graceful as he walked to the window, and she watched, unwillingly, the play of muscles beneath his skin.

"Aren't you cold?" she demanded, unable to stand it any longer.

He glanced over his shoulder at her. "No," he said. "Are you?"

"As a matter of fact, this room is downright chilly."

His dark eyes took on an abstract look. "Interesting," he said. "I was thinking of opening a window."

"How about turning on the heat instead?"

He'd turned back to stare out the window, and something obviously caught his eye. Unable to resist, she rose and joined him, keeping her shoulder away from his as she glanced down at the neat little landscaped yard that adjoined the parking lot.

"What's so interesting?" she demanded, wishing she hadn't moved quite so close, unwilling to betray her discomfort by moving away. One thing was sure—he *was* quite warm. She could feel the heat of his body through the inches of space between them, through her layers of clothing.

"That car down there. I don't remember seeing it before."

"You've memorized all the cars that park here?" she said, disbelieving.

He glanced down at her, and the sensation was unnerving. His gaze was as heated as all that bare skin, which was far too close to hers. "I have that kind of mind," he said. "It doesn't require any effort on my part."

"Maybe there's a new tenant."

"No. Two men were sitting in it, staring up at this building. This window."

"Where are they now?"

"They're over there talking to the security guard. I wonder..."

His voice trailed off as Suzanna leaned forward to get a better look at the two men. She felt her arm brush against his, and she controlled her nervous start. She didn't know what was wrong with her. Men didn't make her nervous. Particularly men like Daniel Crompton, no matter how unexpectedly gorgeous he was turning out to be.

She concentrated on the two men. They were almost ridiculously anonymous, with their dark suits and their bland, middle-aged, middle-class faces. And Daniel was absolutely right—they were in deep conversation with the security guard, and all three of the men were staring directly at their window.

"They've got an out-of-state license plate," she said quietly. "Either that, or it's some sort of official one. I can't quite read it from this distance."

He tilted his head to stare at the gray sedan, focusing intently, and then rubbed his nose absently. "I think it's got Oregon plates," he said after a moment, moving closer, his arm resting against hers. "I can just make them out...." He twitched his elegant nose, staring at the back of the sedan.

The explosion shattered the morning quiet. The shock of it knocked Suzanna back against Daniel, and his hands came up to catch her, holding her against his hot, hard chest for a breathless moment.

She couldn't move. He was burning up, so hot his hands burned through the soft cotton jersey of her

T-shirt, so hot that the smooth skin of his chest scorched her back, so hot that she melted against him, wanting to sink into that heat, lose herself in the glorious warmth of him. And then the glow of the fire down below pulled her out of her momentary weakness, and she jerked herself away, uneasily aware of the fact she hadn't wanted to move at all.

If the touch of her body against his had disturbed him even a fraction as much as it had disturbed her, he didn't show it. He simply leaned past her, looking out the window, a cool, caluclating expression on his face.

"Must be another car bomb," he murmured.

"*Another* car bomb?" Suzanna shrieked, thoroughly rattled. "What are you talking about?"

"The same thing happened when I was walking home this morning. A car exploded." He didn't seem unduly concerned by it all.

"And you think it's a coincidence?" she demanded.

"No." He looked down at her, and there was an unreadable expression in his dark, fire-lit eyes. "I think someone's trying to kill me."

It was such a melodramatic statement, said in such a matter-of-fact tone, but Suzanna could hardly argue with it. Not with the testimony of her own eyes.

"Maybe I don't want to hang around, after all," she said uneasily.

"And miss your chance at the scoop of the century?" he murmured. "Think of the fame and fortune."

"I can't enjoy fame and fortune if I'm caught in the crossfire." She wasn't seriously thinking of wimping out. She'd never been a coward in her life, and she wasn't about to start now. Tempting as the thought might be, she wasn't quite ready to turn her back on Daniel

Crompton, if for no other reason than her insatiable curiosity.

"You think you can protect yourself?" he asked idly, moving away from the window as the resulting chaos of the fire lost his interest.

"Do you think you can protect me?"

"You're probably safer with me, even though it makes things more difficult, as far as I'm concerned." He shrugged. "It's up to you, of course. It makes no difference to me."

The thought rankled. Another man would want to protect her, but then, she'd never been one who needed protection. Still, the man might at least show a trace of concern for her well-being.

"You aren't getting rid of me that easily, Crompton," she said. "I didn't like getting bathed in green slime any more than you did. I'd kind of like to find out who was behind it."

He didn't move for a moment. "Then let's go," he said finally.

He'd managed to startle her. "Go where?"

"To the scene of the crime, of course. If we want answers, Beebe is the place to find them."

At least he'd have to put on a shirt. She viewed that prospect with definite mixed feelings. "I don't suppose you have anything to eat in this place? I'm starving."

"There's some vegamin in the refrigerator."

"What's that? It sounds like bug spray."

He'd disappeared into the bedroom, and she resisted the impulse to tiptoe after him and watch him get dressed. "It's a nutritional drink," he said. "Gives you all the nutrients, and you don't have to bother with food."

"Bother with food?" she echoed, aghast. "Food is one of life's greatest pleasures."

"It's a waste of time," he said, reappearing in the bedroom door. He was buttoning a chambray shirt over his lean, muscled chest, and he'd shoved his feet into a worn pair of high tops. "As a matter of fact, I've been told it tastes like bug spray."

"I think I'll pass. There's a fast-food place on the way. I need coffee."

"I don't suppose you have a car."

"It's out at Beebe."

"So is mine. I guess we run."

"Run?" Suzanna echoed, horrified. "Are you crazy? Nothing short of life or death would make me run. You must be some sort of health fanatic."

"Not particularly. Running enlarges the arteries, which is always beneficial."

"My arteries are just fine," she said firmly. "Let's call a taxi."

"We could walk."

"Taxi," she repeated. "And we'll have him stop on the way."

DANIEL HAD NEVER REALIZED how good he'd be at manipulation. The very stubborn and surprisingly luscious Suzanna Molloy had done exactly as he wanted her to, with only the slightest bit of subtle prodding. There was no way he was going to let her out of his sight, but he knew perfectly well she'd fight that unless she thought it was her idea.

It was simple enough to dangle his cooperation in front of those myopic brown eyes. The fact of the matter was, he was intent on keeping her with him, for a number of reasons. For one thing, she'd been in the same explosion he'd been in, an explosion that seemed to raise his body temperature and give him the uncanny ability to disappear. He didn't know what else he could do, but he suspected his strange side effects weren't at an end. He wanted to see if she was similarly affected.

There was always the chance she was behind that explosion in the lab, though he doubted it. He laid the blame squarely at Henry Osborn's door, and he hadn't missed Suzanna's squirm of discomfort when he brought up his name. Something had happened between them, and Daniel intended to find out what. He also meant to find out who his enemies were, and who were his friends.

And then, of course, there was the little matter of sheer, unbridled lust. Ms. Suzanna Molloy happened to have the uncanny ability to push all the right buttons. He wasn't used to being at the mercy of his physical nature. He drank vegamin to fuel his body, ran to keep his energy at peak, but in general he kept his appetites under rigid control.

Molloy endangered that control. If he had any sense he'd keep away from her, but he wasn't feeling particularly sensible. He was feeling adventuruous, edgy and hot.

And that heat was directed at Suzanna Molloy.

Chapter Five

A couple of hours later, Daniel was still distracted by the woman. He had to admit it—Suzanna Molloy fascinated him. It was a novel situation. There was little that interested him outside of his work, but he was finding the bundle of contradictions that had picked the lock to his apartment to be downright mesmerizing. Enough so that he was almost ready to ignore the question of who or what was behind the sabotage at Beebe.

However, even if he wanted to ignore it and concentrate on Molloy, he doubted whether she'd have any part of it. She seemed to have her own agenda, and she didn't strike him as the sort who'd let anything get in her way.

Daniel Crompton wasn't the sort of man who followed anything but his own inclination. Fortunately, right now his inclination followed quite closely with Suzanna's. He was more than willing to give in to her wishes, as long as they dovetailed with his.

She sat as far away from him as she could in the back of the cab, a foam cup of coffee in one capable-looking hand, some disgusting breakfast concoction in the other. It smelled like eggs and sausage and grease, and she was eating it with obvious relish. He'd given her the approximate cholesterol count when she'd first unwrapped it, but her succinct reply had managed to shock him into silence, even as it amused him. Clearly Ms. Molloy fancied herself one tough lady, from the tips of her black leather running shoes to the top of her silky straight hair. Too bad that the faintly yearning expression in her wonderful eyes betrayed her. Too bad her mouth was deliciously vulnerable when it wasn't curled in hostility.

She didn't like him, he knew that much. But he was also quite certain he could change her mind, if he set himself to do so. The question was, why was he even considering such a thing?

He leaned back in the corner of the cab, inhaling the aroma of coffee and grease and old cigarettes, and he smiled faintly. His behavior was completely uncharacteristic, a fact which disturbed him only slightly. He'd become too predictable in the last few years. He was more than ready to change his ways, and Suzanna Molloy offered him the perfect means to do just that.

"Why are you looking at me like that?" she demanded, delicately licking the grease off her fingers like an elegant cat.

"Like what?"

"You're smirking at me," she said. "I don't trust men who smirk."

She had a trace of shining grease on the side of her mouth. He felt the sudden, irrational urge to kiss her there, to taste it. How very odd. "I'm not smirking," he said with an attempt at severity. "I'm simply smiling. You amuse me."

"You're easily amused." As the taxi approached the front entrance to Beebe Control Systems International, she leaned forward and squinted through her wire-rimmed glasses. "Where's my car?" she demanded suspiciously.

The parking lot was practically empty, which was to be expected on a Saturday morning. For some reason the researchers at Beebe weren't encouraged to work on weekends. "Where did you leave it?" He leaned forward and handed a ten-dollar bill to the long-suffering driver.

"Not far away from that ridiculous car," she said, clambering out of the taxi and staring around her in dismay. It was only a little after nine, and Daniel could see the faint mist rising from the surrounding fields. It was a cool morning, and he still felt hot.

"Which ridiculous car?" he asked evenly. "You mean the Ferrari?"

"Is that what it is? I wouldn't have thought anyone working here could afford such a thing. I can't imagine spending that much on something to drive you to work."

"I can."

She turned to look at him, an arrested expression on her face. "That's your car?"

"It is. I happen to like craftsmanship."

He was half expecting another snotty comment from her. Instead, she merely looked at him, considering. "Isn't it a little small for you? You must have to drive lying down."

"I can do any number of things lying down," he said, keeping his face a perfect blank.

Suspicion darkened her wonderful eyes for a moment, then she clearly dismissed it, unable to believe he would be indulging in even the faintest innuendo. Obviously she didn't think him capable of suggestive remarks. He was capable of a great deal more than that, when so moved, and Suzanna Molloy moved him, more than anyone in his recent memory.

"I want to know where my car is," she said.

"Osborn probably had it towed."

"I'll kill him."

"Bloodthirsty, aren't you? What kind of car did you have? Some yuppie-mobile?"

"Not likely. It's an old wreck that barely runs."

"Then stop whining. If Osborn killed it he'll have to replace it, and Beebe seems to have unlimited money. You play your cards right and you might end up with a Ferrari yourself."

He watched with fascination as she rubbed a surreptitious hand across her breast. He would have been more than happy to do the same, a fact which still surprised him. The heat was rising in his body, and he reached up and unfastened another button of his chambray shirt.

"I don't want a Ferrari, and I'm not the kind of reporter who takes bribes, Dr. Crompton," she said severely. "I want my own car, and I'm not whining."

"Glad to hear it. I'm going in to check on the lab. If you want to keep harping, feel free to stay here. That, or you can come with me."

She was torn, he could see it. He irritated the hell out of her, though he expected that wasn't a difficult task. Anyone who wore a shirt that said Eat Quiche and Die had to have an attitude problem.

That was something that didn't bother him in the slightest. He was generally considered to be socially impaired, though he felt his own particular brand of charm was underrated. He had yet to exert it on Suzanna, and he couldn't help but wonder what her reaction might be. She'd probably offer him quiche.

"I'm coming with you," she said. "We can worry about my car later."

"I knew you were a sensible woman."

NOW WHY DIDN'T SHE LIKE the idea of Daniel Crompton considering her a sensible woman?

The fact that he respected her brain, not her body, was a blessing, wasn't it?

Even if she happened to find him distractingly attractive.

His blue shirt was unbuttoned halfway down his chest, a fact which irritated her. Who did he think he was— some lounge lizard? All he needed was a couple of gold chains to complete the look.

Except that he was far too lean and mean to be a lounge lizard. That bristling intelligence shone in his dark, mesmerizing eyes, twisted his cynical mouth, and his quick, decisive energy wouldn't know the meaning of the word *lounge*.

She just wished he'd button up his damned shirt.

Just as she wished she had a sweater. She'd been cold since she left the hospital, and she should have asked the man for something warmer to wear. Only the fact that she didn't want to wrap herself in any of his clothing had stopped her. He disturbed her, and she wasn't quite sure why. To be sure, he was annoyingly handsome. Condescending, impatient, brilliant, arrogant. There were any number of reasons why she didn't particularly like him.

What she couldn't figure out was why he managed to get to her. She was used to brilliant men, impatient men, and God knows the vast majority of them tended to be arrogant and condescending. It made no sense that she reacted so strongly to Daniel Crompton, and had since she'd first seen him, at a Beebe press conference months ago. If it hadn't been for Uncle Vinnie's inside tip, she would have been more than happy to keep her distance from the man. She didn't like feeling vulnerable.

She could feel the heat emanating from his body. Strange, that. It was a cool day, and yet he was walking around, half-undressed, warmth radiating from his skin, and he wasn't even sweating. She might almost have thought he had a fever, except the man seemed disgustingly healthy.

Maybe he knew the effect he had on her, the irrational attraction that was putting her in such a toweringly bad mood. She wouldn't put it past him. She had only one way to defend herself. Keep as bristly as possible. She might find the man luscious, but that didn't mean she had to betray herself.

She followed Crompton into the anonymous white building, keeping her head down. Even on a Saturday morning with an empty parking lot, the security desk was well manned. She didn't recognize the uniformed guard. Yesterday it had been an elderly man. Today it looked like a Green Beret.

Crompton didn't even bother to slow his headlong pace. He put one of those strong, elegant hands under Suzanna's elbow, and she almost screamed, biting down on her lip to stop her shriek. His flesh was burning hot against her own chilled skin, and it took all her self-control not to jerk away from him.

"Dr. Crompton," the guard growled. "No visitors are allowed on the premises today."

Daniel kept moving. "This isn't a visitor."

"I'm sorry, sir, but she doesn't have security clearance—"

They were already at the elevator. "Of course she does," Crompton snapped. "Do you think I'd bring someone in who'd compromise my work? What kind of fool do you think I am?"

The Green Beret was made of sterner stuff, and he didn't quail in the face of Crompton's biting contempt. "Sir, I'm going to have to ask you to come back while I get clearance for your friend...."

The elevator door swished open. "You get clearance," Daniel said. "We'll stop on our way back." He hauled Suzanna into the elevator, punched the buttons, and a moment later the doors closed and the tiny box began to rise.

Suzanna did not like enclosed spaces. She'd used the stairs yesterday, ostensibly because she was less likely to be caught, but really because she never trusted elevators. The cage began to rise smoothly, and then it jerked to a halt, throwing Suzanna back against the smooth metal walls.

"Damn," Crompton muttered.

Suzanna managed a strained smile, hoping she could fool him. "What happened?"

"I'd think it was obvious. The security guard stopped the elevator."

"Between floors?" She couldn't keep the hollow note out of her voice.

Daniel was busy pushing the various floor buttons, all to no avail. "Not for long. He'll probably try to bring us back down."

Thank God, Suzanna thought devoutly.

"However, I intend to stop him." He shoved open the metal door above the buttons and reached in, coming out with a handful of multicolor wires.

"What do you think you're doing?" They'd already started to descend once more, something she could only view with relief.

"I'm stopping him." He yanked, hard, and the elevator stopped once more. The lights flickered, and then the tiny cage was plunged into claustrophobic darkness.

She thought she did scream then, though in the tiny airless cubicle it came out as nothing more than a helpless whimper. It was pitch-black, airless, smothering, and the heat was suddenly intolerable, an inferno, emanating from Daniel Crompton's dangerously beautiful body.

"Suzanna." His voice was deep, cool and infinitely patient, and she realized distantly that it wasn't the first time he'd said her name. She had backed up against the walls of the elevator, but even the coolness of the metal against her splayed hands couldn't calm her.

"The emergency light," she managed to choke out.

"Doesn't seem to be working." Again that cool, soothing tone. "Are you afraid of the dark?"

It was so cold in there, cold and hot at the same time, like burning ice. She pushed herself harder against the unyielding walls, wishing she could just disappear. "No," she said, trying to sound hostile, knowing that she sounded scared.

He'd crossed the vast, dead space of the pitch-black elevator, and he was standing close, very close. For the first time she didn't find it threatening. The danger from the suffocating darkness was far worse than the danger from one distractingly attractive man.

"Claustrophobic?" he murmured again, coaxing, soothing.

"No," she said, furious that her voice wavered. "I j-j-just don't l-l-l-like elevators."

The touch of his hand on her arm was tentative, gentle, accustoming her to his presence rather than grabbing her out of the darkness like a fiend from hell. She could feel the heat in his fingers, and even in the darkness she could see them—long, elegant, stained with compounds, marked with nicks and scars from long-ago experiments. She wanted those hands on her, holding her against the smothering darkness. She needed those hands on her.

When he pulled her into his arms she didn't even pretend to resist, just closed off her brain, with all its doubts and anger, all its warnings. She sank against Daniel Crompton's fiery body, absorbing the heat, and shut her eyes, as his hand cupped the back of her head and pushed her face against his shoulder, gently, protectively.

A tiny mutinous part of her cried out that she didn't need protecting. But that part was quickly silenced, as she absorbed his heat, his strength and his comfort. As her panicked heartbeat began to slow, the icy chill of fear left her, and she was able to breathe once more.

He seemed to know moments before she did that she needed to pull away. When he released her, the darkness slammed about her once more, but this time she could cope. She took a deep breath, willing the panic to retreat.

"Better now?" His voice was infinitely pragmatic, as if holding her in his arms was a commonplace occurrence.

"Fine," she said, wishing she could have put a little more edge into her voice. Though she suspected, even in the darkness, that she couldn't fool him. "Can we get the hell out of here?"

"Certainly." She heard a rustling in the darkness, a muffled, shifting noise that made her want to scream. A moment later a square of pale light appeared in the ceiling, and she could see Crompton's vague outline.

"You first," he said. "Unless you're afraid of heights, as well."

"I'm not afraid of anything," she shot back, an obvious lie. "What do you mean, me first?"

"If you want to get out of this elevator, there's only one way, and that's up."

"I'm not about to—"

"It's up," he said ruthlessly, "or stay here for what will probably be another two hours. And you'll do it alone. I'm out of here."

"You know what I like about you, Dr. Crompton?" she asked in a silken voice that almost masked her panic.

"No, what?"

"Absolutely nothing."

As a matter of fact, she wasn't particularly crazy about heights. She was even less fond of climbing upward through a narrow, constricted tube, above an object that might suddenly start moving and end up squashing her against the ceiling of the building like a fat bug.

But she wasn't about to spend a minute longer in that elevator than she had to. Particularly not alone.

"Get me out of here, Crompton," she muttered, moving toward him, perversely glad that the darkness hid the expression on her face.

"Up you go," he said, putting his big, hot hands on her waist and hoisting her upward with a total effortlessness that just managed to get through her fear enough to astonish her. She reached out instinctively as he pushed her through the opening, his hands sliding down her hips to cup her rear before she managed to grab hold of something and scramble out of his way.

A moment later he'd vaulted up beside her, and in the improved light she could see his eyes gleaming in the shadows. "That was easy enough."

"Too easy, Crompton. I weigh a hundred and thirty-seven pounds."

"That's not my fault, Molloy. You eat too much grease."

It would be a waste of time to hit him. She could at least wait until he'd gotten her out of this place. "I mean you don't seem the slightest bit strained."

"I'm used to lifting weights."

The hell with waiting, she *was* going to hit him. "We're not talking about a male-dominated distortion of aesthetics, Dr. Crompton," she said icily. "We're talking about—"

"Why are we wasting our time talking? I thought you wanted to get out of here."

"I do."

"Then stop complaining about your weight and follow me."

She spent a moment fondly contemplating his immediate demise, when light began to stream into the elevator shaft. It took her a moment to realize he'd reached over his head and was prying open the doors to the next floor.

Well, maybe she wouldn't kill him after all. Just hurt him very badly.

"Climb up," he offered.

"I'll need a hand."

"The doors will close again."

"I can pry them open. I may not lift weights, but I'm far from a weak woman."

"I never made the mistake of assuming you were weak. Nevertheless, you wouldn't be able to open them yourself. Climb up."

"But how...?"

"Use my body," he said blandly.

The suggestion was startling, until she realized what he meant. "I don't know..."

"Listen, I want to get out of here as much as you do, and I'd like to do it before they get someone in here who can override the system and make this thing start up again. Now move your butt, Molloy, or I'll move it for you."

She'd hurt him with a great deal of pain, she thought fondly, reaching out to touch him. He was hot, something which didn't surprise her. The odd thing was, his clothes were cool to the touch.

She could feel the tension in his muscles. It was an unnerving experience, but as far as she could see, she really had no choice. "All right," she said in a tight little voice. "How do you expect me to do this?"

"Grab hold of my shoulders and start climbing."

He hadn't tied his hair back, and it brushed against her fingers as she settled them on his shoulders, the cool chambray beneath her hands. He was holding very still, keeping the doors open, his arms directly overhead. "I don't think this is going to work," she said, biting her lip.

"Think how much fun you're going to have, stomping all over me. Use your feet, Molloy."

She braced one sneakered foot against his leg, her fingers digging into the bunched-up shoulder muscles, and tried to hoist herself up. Her knee slammed into his stomach, her foot came perilously close to his groin, and the feel of his iron-hard body beneath hers was incredibly distracting.

He was wearing a wide leather belt, and she managed to rest her foot against it, pushing herself upward. Her stomach was face level, and she could feel the warmth of his breath against the zipper of her jeans. Her foot slipped, and she fell against him, his face buried in her crotch.

It didn't take his muffled laughter to send her flying upward through the pried-open doors, belly-flopping onto the carpet. She scrambled out of the way, rolling over in time to see him follow her, just as the door slammed shut behind him.

The power was out in the hall, as well, but the midday sun managed to send squares of light into the corridor, and Suzanna sank back, drinking in the diffuse brightness of the day and the blessed feel of the floor beneath her. "Was that, by any chance, a pass, Molloy?" he inquired.

"Go to hell, Dr. Crompton," she said, pulling herself upright. He was standing there in the shadowed hallway, tall, superior, a gleam of mocking humor in his dark eyes. Now was the time to kill him.

"Let's get moving," he said, reaching out a hand. "We probably won't have much time before Beebe's private army arrives."

She looked up at him. His shirt had come unbuttoned, pulled out of his jeans, and she remembered the feel of his skin beneath her clutching hands. "Maybe I'll wait to kill you," she muttered, putting her hand in his outstretched one.

His was much larger. It closed around hers, warm and strong, and he pulled her to her feet.

"That might be wise," he murmured. "Not much farther, Nancy Drew. Come on."

And he left her to race after him down the hallway, once she'd gotten over her initial shock.

Chapter Six

This situation was getting more and more interesting, Daniel thought, moving down the darkened hallway at a brisk pace. Despite his ongoing fascination with his research project, he found he'd gotten into a rut recently. Certainly the last twenty-four hours had provided enough novelty to keep him entertained for the next twenty-four years.

He was immensely strong. It had taken very little effort to pry open those pneumatic doors, very little to send Suzanna's well-rounded figure up and over the portal and into the hall. Levering himself after her had also been surprisingly simple. He wished he had a moment to experiment further, but he wasn't about to do that with an audience. He wanted to keep Suzanna with him, but he wasn't quite ready to share what was going on with his body.

Fortunately she seemed willing to accompany him, though he didn't have any illusions about her motives. She wanted the truth. She wanted a story, a scoop, and she'd betray him in a flash if she had to. He had no intention of giving her the chance.

He opened the fire door to the staircase. "Think you can handle this?" he asked. "The emergency lights are out here, as well."

"When you pull the plug you don't settle for halfway measures, do you?" she said. "I can do it." She moved past him, into the enveloping darkness of the hallway, and as her body brushed by he could smell the faint trace of soap that clung to her. It was surprisingly erotic.

He let the door swing shut behind him, following her up the stairs in the inky darkness. He could see her quite clearly, hear her struggle to control her nervous breathing as she climbed, slowly, steadily, her hand clutching the metal stair rail.

"You're there, aren't you?" she called out, her voice betraying only a trace of her nerves.

"Right behind you," he said, wondering why she couldn't see him when he could see her quite clearly.

She'd paused, and she was staring in his direction in the darkness, but her own gaze was unfocused. "Your eyes . . ." she said.

Instinctively he closed his lids. "What about them?"

"Nothing," she mumbled. "Must have been my imagination." He heard her turn away and continue to mount the stairs, and he waited a moment before he followed her. What had she seen in his eyes?

The third floor smelled of smoke and chemicals. The hallway was deserted, though at the far end he could see the rubble that had once been his doorway. A yellow tape stretched in front of it, though Daniel doubted that there'd been a police investigation.

Suzanna's color was decidedly pale, though she looked happier to be out of the darkness. "How much time do you think we've got?"

"Probably not enough," he said, moving past her. "I just want to take a quick look around, see if I can find out what kind of device they used, and then we're out of here."

"Device? You sound pretty certain it was sabotage."

He glanced at her, one part of his mind taking in the way the T-shirt clung to her breasts and remembering the feel of her body as she'd scrambled up him, the rest being coldly analytical. "I don't make mistakes," he said simply.

"Never?"

He paused long enough to consider it. "Not that I can remember."

The lab was a shambles. It stank of chemicals, of smoke, of fire extinguisher foam and wet, charred wood and melted plastic. Most of the green slime had been washed away by the fire hoses, but a little pool of the stuff remained under one of the workbenches, and he squatted down, staring at it for a long time before he scooped some up in a plastic dish he'd brought along for the purpose.

"Why are you doing that?" Suzanna was leaning over his shoulder, close enough to touch him. "Do you think that stuff caused the explosion?"

"No." He rose, coming up beside her, near enough to touch her if he wanted to. He wanted to. "I think it's a by-product of what I was working on, combined with whatever was used to start the fire. It's mutated into something that I intend to identify." He tucked the plastic dish in his hip pocket. "Did you get any of the stuff on you?"

"Just a little. You took a bath in it."

"So I did," he murmured. "I wonder—" He stopped. "They're coming."

"I don't hear anything."

"Don't you? They're coming up the north stairwell—about two flights down. I'd say we have about one minute at the most."

"You can't hear them that far away!" she snapped, but he could see the definite alarm in her beautiful brown eyes.

"Trust me," he muttered, taking her hand in his and starting out of the ruined lab at a run.

For once she didn't argue. She simply followed him, no questions asked, as he dodged debris, racing down the deserted hallway on silent feet.

He darted into Buchanan's lab, slamming the door behind them and closing them in shadowy darkness. Buchanan had left several months ago, and the lab had sat empty since then, despite Daniel's best efforts to co-opt it for his own uses. Not that it was as large as Daniel's lab, but it came equipped with a back staircase, leading directly to the roof.

"Where are we going?" Suzanna finally demanded, breathless. "Why are we running? You don't think we're in any real danger, do you?"

He thought there was a good chance that they were in a great deal of danger, but he wasn't about to explain it to a nosy reporter. "I don't know. I just want to get out of here. Call me paranoid."

"You're paranoid."

He turned to look at her. "You want to wait around for them to come find you?"

"I have a T-shirt that says Just Because You're Paranoid Doesn't Mean They Aren't Out To Get You," she replied.

"Good girl," he muttered, moving toward the door at the back of the lab.

"Don't call me a girl," she snapped, moving past him and reaching for the metal doorknob. Of course it didn't budge, and she yanked harder, muttering under her breath. "I don't suppose you have a key for this?"

"No."

"Then we're stuck." She turned and glared at him, her wheat-blond hair tumbling into her eyes. "That's a safety door—reinforced steel. Unless you can pick locks, there's no way we're going to get past it. Brute force just won't cut it this time."

"I wonder," he said, half to himself, moving past her, ignoring the impractical urge to touch her. He took hold of the shiny steel knob, noting the lock. And then he turned it, crushing the tumblers when they tried to resist, pulling open the door with no effort whatsoever.

She stared at him for a moment, then back at the door latch. The metal workings had been pulverized by some massive force. "How did you do that?" she gasped.

"Shoddy workmanship," he replied. "You first. Three flights up, and if the door's locked up there, we'll open it."

Her parting glance was wary, before she vanished into the shadowy staircase. Daniel watched her for a moment, appreciating the curve of her rear in the faded jeans, before he turned to look at the door. His strength was quite impressive. He really needed to get out of here, away from witnesses, and experiment further. There had to be a limit to it, and he needed to find that limit. He didn't want to accidently injure someone.

He stepped into the narrow staircase, pulling the damaged door shut behind him, hoping it would escape detection, at least for the time being. He could hear Suzanna moving upward, her sneakered feet cautious. She was nervous again, the darkness of the passageway getting to her, and he told himself he ought to catch up with her, hold her hand, even put his arm around her. Just to reassure her, he told himself virtuously. Hell, given his unpredictable strength, he could carry her the rest of the way and barely notice the burden. He rather liked that idea.

There was an odd, sickly sweet smell in the stairwell, not unlike rancid meat and rotted fruit. The higher he climbed, the stronger the stench, and he wondered what Suzanna was doing, why he could no longer hear her tentative footsteps, her nervous breathing, why she wasn't complaining.

He found her on the landing just before the final flight of stairs to the roof. She wasn't alone.

She was standing utterly motionless. The skylight overhead illuminated the area, but Daniel doubted she was grateful for the light. It shone down on the corpse of Robert Jackson.

"Is he dead?" Suzanna's voice came out as no more than a whisper.

Daniel stepped farther, intellectually gratified at having identified the stench. "Most definitely," he said. "Don't you see the bullet hole in his—"

"Please!" Suzanna begged in a strangled voice.

"Why don't you go on up ahead? I'll be right with you."

"What are you going to do?"

"Search his body. You want to help?"

She disappeared up the final flight of stairs with a quiet shriek of protest. When he reached her side a few moments later, she was leaning against the locked fire door, her hand over her mouth, her eyes wide behind the wire-rimmed glasses.

"Are you going to throw up?" He was unalarmed at the notion, simply curious.

"No." She took a deep, shuddering breath. "Can we get out of here? This door is locked, as well, and I've checked. It's very solidly put together."

"You'd be surprised." He tempered his strength this time, turning the knob just enough to break the lock, not enough to pulverize it. He opened the door for her, pushing her through into the fresh air before she could look too closely.

He started across the deserted rooftop at a fast pace. "Come on," he said. "If our luck holds, we'll be out of here before they realize it."

"And if it doesn't?"

"We might end up like Jackson back there."

Wrong words. She swayed for a moment, and her pale face looked even chalkier. He started back, ready to catch her if she fell, but she managed to straighten her back and square her shoulders. "Not if I have anything to say about it," she muttered.

"Good girl."

"Stop saying that. I'm not a girl."

"Argue with me once we're out of here," he said. "In the meantime, get your delectable butt in gear."

SUZANNA WOULDN'T HAVE thought Daniel Crompton was the sort of man who noticed butts, delectable or otherwise. No one had ever referred to that part of her anatomy in such flattering terms, and she concentrated on that, rather than the vision, the smell, of the dead man in the stairwell, as she followed Crompton over the side of the building and down a metal fire ladder to a deserted parking lot.

Or almost deserted. There was a Jaguar parked there, sleek, forest green and Suzanna's dream car, and she stared at it for a moment when she reached the ground, a wave of covetousness sweeping over her.

"If we're going to steal a car, I opt for that one," she said.

Crompton looked at her. The man was inhuman. He seemed to accept decaying corpses as nothing more than an intellectual exercise, he didn't recognize such a thing as a locked door, and she was beginning to get the feeling that there was something very different about Dr. Daniel Crompton. That first stretch of hallway had been eerie enough. Trapped in the suffocating darkness, she'd turned back, looking for some kind of companionship, and had found only a pair of eyes glowing in the darkness.

It had to have been her imagination. In the inky darkness she could barely see his silhouette, and that odd shining had disappeared in a moment.

Still, she'd tried both of those steel doors. While she'd never pretended to be a superwoman, she had a certain amount of strength, and those doors were locked tight. Yet Crompton had opened them with no visible effort whatsoever.

"Who says we're stealing a car?"

"I don't know where mine is, and they'll be watching yours," she pointed out. "It doesn't take someone with your exalted IQ to figure out that much."

"That Jaguar belongs to Henry Osborn, and he's formidable enough without us taking his precious car. We're taking the Ford over there."

Suzanna followed his gaze. It was a boring enough vehicle, two door, late model, indiscriminate color. They'd probably blend in well enough, if that was their wish. "I'd still rather have the Jag," she said, trotting along behind him.

Of course the car was locked. She stood at the passenger door, throwing him a mocking glance. "Are you going to rip the door off the hinges this time?" she murmured.

"It might be easier to simply unlock it," he said, pulling a set of keys from his pocket and doing so. She slid into the front seat beside him, rolling down her window to let some of the suffocatingly stale air out, as Crompton started the car and pulled out of the parking lot at an impressive speed. Even with the wind blowing through the open window it was too hot. It took her a moment to remember she was keeping company with a human furnace.

"If this isn't your car, whose is it? How'd you happen to get the keys?" she demanded, fastening the seat belt around her.

"I don't think you want to know."

Horror swept over her. "It isn't!"

Daniel shrugged. "Jackson isn't going to need it anymore. It was simple enough to find his keys."

She looked down at the set hanging from the ignition. The key ring had a shamrock hanging from it. It certainly hadn't provided much luck for the late Jackson. "You're sick," she said, sinking back against the seat.

"Just practical. Speaking of which, I think we'd better get out of town for a while."

"Why?"

"Because this isn't just a case of industrial sabotage or attempted murder. Someone actually managed to kill Jackson, and whoever it was used a fair amount of detail and imagination. I don't think they're going to stop there. Where do you live?"

"Why?"

"I thought you might want to pick up some clothes. Assuming they're not watching your place."

"What makes you think I'm going with you?"

"Molloy, you've got it made. You're in on a murder. Think of the bidding wars on your movie rights."

"Sorry, Crompton, you haven't got hero potential," she snapped, ignoring the fact that he was better-looking than almost any actor she could think of.

"Who says I'm not the villain?"

That managed to silence her. It was a startling thought. She'd gone along with him, arguing, but trusting, putting her life in his hands. Together they'd found Jackson's body, and yet Daniel had looked at it as if it were nothing more than a lab experiment gone awry.

Could he have killed him? Did he find out that Jackson had tried to sabotage his lab, and shoot him in a rage? She glanced over at his profile. His long hair blew in the wind, away from his strong-featured face. He looked cool, remote, incapable of human emotion. If he ever wanted to kill someone, he was smart enough to get away with it.

"43 West Peacock."

He glanced over at her. "I beg your pardon?"

"You asked where I lived. It's 43 West Peacock. Just off of High Street."

"Does that mean you're coming with me?"

"As you pointed out, it's the scoop of the century. I'm going to be your shadow."

His mouth curved in a faint, mocking smile. "You might find that harder than you think."

"I can rise to the challenge. Do you know where we're going?"

"Somewhere I can think. You don't talk all the time, do you?"

"Depends on my mood."

"God help me," he muttered. But for some reason he didn't look the slightest bit distressed.

As far as they could tell, no one was watching the old Victorian-style house where she rented her apartment. Crompton stayed in the car while she ran inside and filled an old duffel bag with a dozen T-shirts, all the clean underwear she could find and enough toiletries to keep her human. She yanked her clothes off, throwing them in the trash, and quickly pulled on a new T-shirt and jeans. It was ridiculous, but she felt as if the smell of that long-dead corpse was clinging to her. The sooner she could take a long hot shower, the better.

Daniel was waiting for her in the sedan, his long fingers drumming on the steering wheel. "You're fast," he said approvingly. "You even managed to change your clothes."

"I try not to waste time."

"Nice T-shirt," he said, pulling out into the late afternoon traffic.

She glanced down at the one she'd grabbed. So Many Men, So Few Bullets, it read, in black ink on a red background. She thought back to Jackson and shivered.

He headed out onto the highway, moving north into the mountains. She sank back against the cushions, closing her eyes in sudden exhaustion. She must have drifted off, for the next thing she knew, they were parked outside of a very seedy-looking motel, somewhere in the middle of nowhere, and the digital clock on the dashboard read 5:40.

"Where are we?" she asked with a yawn.

"On the back side of beyond," he said. "I've got us a room for the night. I've been driving around, doubling back, and I don't think they're likely to find us. We're Mr. and Mrs. Smith."

"How original. We're sharing a room?"

She might almost have wished he'd responded with a leer. Instead he simply looked surprised. "I thought the intention of this was to keep each other alive. We can't do that if you're in another room."

"Don't worry, Dr. Crompton," she said wearily. "I'm not accusing you of having lustful designs on my fair body."

He didn't even blink. A token protest wouldn't have done her ego any harm, but Daniel wasn't adept in the art of social lies. He simply stared at her for a moment. "Do you want me to?" he asked bluntly.

It was getting dark. A fortunate thing, since her damnably fair skin heated up at his artless question. "No," she said flatly.

He nodded. "I see," he said. Something about his tone of voice wasn't particularly reassuring, but before she could identify what it was that bothered her, he'd climbed out of the car and headed for the door of their room.

She grabbed her duffel bag and followed him, telling herself she was glad the big oaf was totally lacking in chauvinistic manners. "Room number thirteen," she noted, stepping inside. "Just our luck."

"What's wrong with number thirteen?"

She didn't bother enlightening him—she was too busy surveying the room in dismay.

At least there were two beds. The place was decorated in early American tacky, from the orange quilted bedspreads to the Naugahyde furniture. She checked beyond, to the tiny square of bathroom with its stall shower, and sighed. "All the comforts of home," she said. "I wonder where Norman Bates is."

"Who's Norman Bates?"

"Didn't you ever see *Psycho?*"

"No."

She shook her head again. "For a brilliant man, Dr. Crompton, you're amazingly ignorant."

If he heard her, he ignored the remark and busily closed the curtains against the gathering darkness. "It's hot in here," he said in a low voice.

Oddly enough, a chill swept over Suzanna's body. "I'm going to take a shower," she said, dumping her duffel bag on the bed nearest the bathroom and rummaging through it.

He had a strained look to him, almost haunted. "Go right ahead."

She paused in the bathroom doorway. "Are you all right?"

"Fine. Take your shower. Then we can see about finding something to eat."

There was something wrong. The room was almost suffocating, and heat emanated from the man at the window. He refused to look at her, and she shrugged. "It's almost six now," she said. "I'll be ready to go out at six-thirty."

"Fine," he said in a muffled voice. "Take your shower."

HE WAITED UNTIL THE DOOR shut behind her. The pain was lancing through his body—intense, sweeping shafts of agony. He heard the water running, the sound of it hitting her body as she stepped beneath the spray, and then he let go, sinking down on the bed as the shivering swept over him. He closed his eyes for a moment, then opened them again. He stared down at his legs, but they were vague, out of focus, and he knew it had happened again.

Once more he was invisible. And he didn't know how in hell he was going to explain that to Suzanna Molloy.

Chapter Seven

Daniel Crompton had been properly reared, the only child of elderly, intellectual parents. His mother had very strict rules of propriety, and even as a toddler he'd been expected to behave as a gentleman. At the advanced age of thirty-four he knew perfectly well that he ought to leave the room and return when he was once more visible.

He wasn't going to.

"I'm going out," he called through the closed bathroom door. "I'll be back in a couple of hours." He heard her sputtered protests as he walked heavily to the front door, opened it, and closed it quite loudly. And then he moved, his sneakered feet silent, to the very corner of the room and sat down gingerly on the bed.

"Crompton, don't you dare leave me!" Suzanna shrieked, sticking her head out of the bathroom door. Her hair was wet, she didn't have her glasses on, and her brown eyes focussed myopically around the confined space, moving past the spot where he sat patiently, not lingering. "Damn the man," she muttered, moving back into the bathroom, leaving the door ajar.

He wondered idly whether he could get up, move across the room and peer inside the bathroom door without her hearing him. He'd never had any voyeuristic tendencies—even when he was a hormone-crazed teenager he'd been more interested in the anatomical anomalies of the centerfolds than their unlikely charms.

But he found he had a sudden urge to see what Suzanna Molloy looked like under her T-shirt. Whether she was curved and soft, sleek and muscled, or a combination of the two. Oddly enough, it didn't really matter to him. For some reason he wanted her—whether she was plump or lean. It was her brown eyes, her stubborn mouth, her wary nature that turned him on. It made no sense, but then, little had in the last twenty-four hours.

He'd just risen when she came back out of the bathroom, and he had to bite back the groan of disappointment. She was already partly dressed, wearing a plain white pair of panties and a T-shirt that read When God Made Man She Was Only Kidding. Her hair was combed back from her freshly scrubbed face, and she was wearing her glasses once more. He froze, afraid to give away his presence, and looked at her.

Come to think of it, maybe he wasn't disappointed. She had long legs, beautiful legs, not Barbie doll legs but the kind that could wrap around a man. She hadn't bothered with a bra, and the T-shirt clung to her wet body, her wet breasts, and he watched her, wishing he could see her nipples, cursing because the room was too warm.

She had an elegant grace when she thought no one was watching her, and she crossed to the door to put the chain up. "Where is that man?" she muttered underneath her breath, peering out the window. Of course, there was no sign of him, and he watched, wondering what else she was going to say.

She moved over to the mirror that hung above the cheap pine dresser. It should have reflected his own body, as well, but it didn't. He stood there, seeing what she was seeing, judging what she was judging.

"All right," she said out loud, pulling her hair back away from her face. "So you're no great beauty. No one ever said you were."

He was tempted to disagree, but he wisely kept his peace, wanting to hear more. "And just because the great Dr. Daniel Crompton happens to be unfairly blessed with more than his fair share of looks, it hasn't got a thing to do with you. At least I don't have to look at him for a while. Pretty is as pretty does, and the man is overbearing, cold-blooded and arrogant."

He wondered about that. It seemed a fairly accurate assessment. He did tend to be overbearing—otherwise he wasted too much time trying not to tread on the tender feelings of utter fools. Arrogant... perhaps. He knew what he wanted, what he was interested in and what bored him. What interested him right now was Suzanna Molloy. Not to mention the strange things that kept happening to his body. But oddly enough, he found his oblivious roommate a higher priority.

As for his being cold-blooded, that seemed to have changed recently, in more ways than one. He was hot, burning up, with a kind of dry heat that could set something on fire. And he was even hotter when he looked at her.

Even if he was invisible, his body was capable of reacting humanly enough. Staring at her breasts in the mirror, he found he was getting aroused. That was odd, as well. He usually got turned on when he had a naked, willing woman in his bed. His erections, his lovemaking, as well as everything else, were always ruthlessly efficient.

Not tonight, however. He shifted his jeans, deciding he might be better off sitting down on the bed. He lowered himself slowly, silently, gingerly, then realized with sudden horror that the reflection of the orange quilted bedspread suddenly wrinkled.

Suzanna froze. She whipped around, staring at the spot where he sat motionless on the bed, and for such a fierce young woman she looked scared spitless.

"Daniel?" she managed to croak.

He didn't say a word. If he could just hold himself still, she'd probably decide she'd imagined it. Except that the quilt was bunched up beneath him, and if she tried to straighten it, she'd run right into him.

"You're here, aren't you?" She moved toward him, and he had to admire her courage in the face of her controlled panic. "I don't know how, but you're here, in the room. I can feel you watching me. Say something, damn it!"

Still he kept silent. She'd be better off not knowing. There was no guarantee he could keep her from Osborn, Armstead and their nasty crew, and if they found out what had happened to him, things would go from bad to worse.

It was more than obvious what Beebe Control Systems International wanted from him, and he'd been a fool to blind himself to their machinations. People didn't kill for patents and copyrights, they didn't sabotage labs and risk killing their major researcher, unless they decided they had what they needed.

What they needed was something they could use to control the world, and they thought he had it. They thought he was the one man who'd finally created cold fusion. And they weren't going to use it to solve the world's energy crisis. They were going to use it for weapons.

When the stakes were that high, the lives of two little people didn't mean a hill of beans. He'd heard that line somewhere—he couldn't remember where—but it seemed to fit. The less Suzanna Molloy knew, the better.

But the problem was, she looked as if she was about to cry, and he knew she wasn't the sort of woman who cried easily or often. The thought of her tears didn't distress him any more than the possibility of her throwing up after she found Jackson's body. He wasn't the kind of man who fell apart at the sight of a woman's tears.

But for some reason he didn't want to see her cry.

"I'm going crazy," she whispered to herself in sudden panic. "I've got to get out of here." She dived for her duffel bag, dragging out a pair of jeans, and it took all his self-control not to leap for her, to try to stop her. He was counting on her to calm herself down, so he wouldn't have to reveal himself, when the utilitarian black phone beside the bed shrilled.

It startled her into a quiet scream; it startled him into moving. He saw the shift of the mattress in the mirror, but Suzanna was too busy staring at the phone.

She started toward it, and he knew he had to stop her. It might very well be only the desk clerk, but he doubted it. They'd been found already.

Her hand was on the receiver, hesitating, when he finally spoke.

"Don't answer it," he said.

He couldn't see her face now, just her straight back, the tension in her shoulders. And then she moved her hand, turned and stared at the empty beds. "Where are you?" she asked with remarkable calm.

He rose. She was still staring at the disarranged bed—she didn't know he was coming closer, close enough to touch her, close enough to pull her into his arms.

He resisted the impulse, but just barely. She'd been through enough, and he was about to put her through more. "Right here," he said softly.

And Suzanna Molloy, tough and fearless, collapsed in a dead faint at his feet.

IT GAVE HIM A CHANCE to experiment. He knelt down beside her, sliding his arms under her limp body, and lifted her up. He might have been lifting a cloud of silk, and yet he knew by looking that Suzanna Molloy was a solidly built young lady. She smelled of shampoo and soap and toothpaste, clean and fresh and unbearably erotic, and he wondered just how conscienceless he was becoming. She was out cold, and he was sorely tempted to—

Her eyes fluttered open. He was carrying her toward the bed, and he could feel her muscles stiffen in his arms, and knew she was about to scream. He couldn't blame her. As far as she could see, she was floating through the air.

He dropped her down on the bed, abruptly enough to surprise the scream out of her. She stared up at him, or at least, in his general direction, and the look of absolute horror on her face was far from flattering.

"I thought you were glad you didn't have to look at me," he said.

She jumped, startled. "Where are you?"

"Standing right in front of you." He wanted to touch her again, but he wasn't sure whether she could handle it or not. Her nerves seemed to be on the ragged edge, and while he didn't usually waste time worrying about other people's needs, in this case it seemed to matter.

"What happened to you?"

He wandered over to the window, glancing out into the night. "I don't know," he said honestly. "It has something to do with the lab accident. The green slime, I suppose. It certainly wasn't anything I was working on."

Her head moved, her eyes following the direction of his voice. "This isn't the first time it's happened?"

He smiled. She was sharp—he liked that about her. Almost as much as he liked her long legs and her breasts and her feisty tongue. "It happened this morning. Six o'clock this morning, to be exact. It lasted exactly two hours, and at eight o'clock I was visible again."

"You were there when I broke into your apartment."

"Yes."

"You were watching me. God, I bumped into you!" she said, remembering.

"Yes," he said again.

"You weren't going to tell me?" Her temper was returning, the color rising in her pale cheeks. "Were you just going to sit there and watch me undress, you pervert?"

"Hardly a pervert. An interest in an unclothed female body of certain attractions isn't the slightest bit abnormal."

"Certain attractions?" she echoed, reacting just as he'd expected.

"Besides, I'm not certain how much I can trust you. Who's to say you won't go to the *National Enquirer* and sell your story?"

"They wouldn't believe me," she said flatly. "Even tabloids have some standards. What else?"

"What do you mean by that?"

"There's more than being invisible. You broke those doors at Beebe, didn't you? And what about the elevator door?"

"I seem to be fairly strong," he allowed.

"How strong? Arnold Schwarzenegger strong? The Incredible Hulk strong? Godzilla strong?"

"I'm not sure. I'm still finding out exactly what's going on," he said, turning to stare at her. She still wasn't wearing a bra, a fact which had temporarily escaped her. The jeans she'd pulled on were a tighter fit than the ones she'd worn earlier, and they encased her long legs. He sighed.

"What do you want from me?" she asked quietly.

"What makes you think I want anything from you?"

"Don't try to trick me, Dr. Crompton. You may have an IQ of 512, but that doesn't mean the rest of us are idiots. You brought me along for a reason. What is it?"

He considered it—and her—for a long moment. "You want the truth?"

She nodded, pushing her damp hair away from her face. "It's usually for the best."

He moved back, across the room, stopping in front of her. "There are a number of reasons."

She jumped when he spoke, startled. "Can't you stay put?" she demanded wtih some asperity. "I can't see you, you know."

"You'll have to get used to me sneaking up on you."

"Charming," she snapped. "Why did you bring me along?"

He decided to be efficient. "Number one," he said, counting on unseen fingers, "I wasn't sure which side you were on. Your arrival at Beebe was, to say the least, suspicious. I thought you might have been behind the lab explosion, and it would be better to have you in sight."

"I wish I could say the same for you," she muttered. "What else?"

"Number two," he said, "you were slimed as well as I was, though you didn't get as thorough a coating. I wanted to see whether you were affected, as well. Number three, I need someone to help me observe the changes in my body, document them. They might prove debilitating, even fatal. I'll need someone I can count on to record them. You're a scientific reporter—I can trust you to keep track of what's happening to me."

"Is that all?" She didn't look particularly gratified at the trust he'd shown her, but then, he wasn't expecting gratitude.

"There are other considerations," he said in his most offhand voice. "I wasn't sure if you already knew what was happening to me, and I didn't want you telling anyone about it. We're better off keeping it a secret, at least for now."

"And?"

"And what?"

"Any other reason?"

None apart from overwhelming animal lust, he thought to himself, smiling wryly. He didn't think Suzanna was ready to hear that. "Isn't that enough?"

"Who says I want to be your dogsbody?" she demanded.

"You've got one of the major qualifications," he said smoothly. "Your nature."

To his surprise, her face creased in reluctant amusement. "Are you by any chance calling me a bitch, Dr. Crompton?" she asked. "You must admit, I have plenty of reason to be irritable."

"Aren't you always this way?"

"You bring out the worst in me." She pulled her legs up underneath her, and he could see she was beginning to lose her wariness. He wondered if she'd lose it enough to let him touch her. He doubted it.

"I wouldn't get too comfortable if I were you," he said.

She stiffened. "What do you mean?"

"I don't know who was calling here, but I don't like it. I think we'd better leave. And you're going to have to drive."

She cocked her head. "I suppose I am. I suppose I'm going to have to carry the bags, as well?"

He nodded, then realized she couldn't see. "I think being invisible will have its advantages."

"How long is it going to last?"

"A reasonably educated guess would say two hours. That's how long it lasted this morning. I disappeared at 6:00 a.m., reappeared at eight. I disappeared at 6:00 p.m. tonight, so I imagine..." He glanced down at his arm, but the watch attached to his wrist was just as blurred and out of focus as the rest of him.

She seemed to guess what his problem was. "It's seven-fifteen. If you're right, that would give you another forty-five minutes." She rose, and if the hand that pushed her damp hair away from her face trembled slightly, she ignored it. "You're right, let's get out of here. I don't suppose you have any idea where we can go?"

"Keep heading in the same general direction. I had a destination in mind."

"You feel like sharing it?"

"Not particularly. That way you won't know anything if we get separated."

"Charming," she said, slipping her feet into her sneakers. "They can torture me, but I won't be able to tell them anything."

"You've been reading too many bad books. Nobody's going to torture anyone."

"It didn't look as if your friend Jackson had too good a time," she snapped. And then she closed her eyes, suddenly looking vulnerable. "I shouldn't have said that."

"Why not? It's true. For what it's worth, Jackson didn't deserve what happened to him, but he wasn't an innocent victim, either. He was somebody's spy, probably Osborn's, and I wouldn't be surprised if he set the device that almost killed the both of us."

"Nevertheless, he was a human being, and he didn't deserve to die like that," she said sternly, grabbing her duffel bag and reaching for his bag, too.

"Working on your sainthood, Molloy? It'll take more than that to convince me."

She opened the door, patiently waiting for him. "I don't need to convince you, Dr. Crompton. You weren't blessed with many human qualities to begin with, and what little you had seems to have disappeared with the rest of you." She smiled sweetly. "It's just a shame you didn't lose your voice, as well."

He couldn't very well argue with her. The door was open, the light overhead illuminating her dark blond hair, illuminating the supposedly empty room. He had no choice but to follow her. He couldn't even close the door behind him. Not with the desk clerk staring out, insatiably curious.

"Are you going to take care of the doors?" he demanded, as she settled into the driver's seat with seeming ease.

"Damn," she said, scooting back out to slam the motel door, then moving around to open the passenger door for him. He knew she was coming, and he deliberately didn't move, letting her barrel into him, catching her arms in his strong hands, letting her chest rest against his.

He'd unbuttoned his shirt against the incessant heat of his body, and her breasts through the thin cotton jersey were hard, pebbled, and he knew damned well it wasn't from the cold. She jerked away, rattled, and he was just as glad she couldn't see his face. She'd already warned him she didn't like it when he smirked, and he had little doubt he had a full-fledged smirk across his face.

"Tell me when you're in," she said between her teeth. "I wouldn't want to slam the door on your foot."

He climbed in quickly, knowing she'd probably be tempted to do just that. "All set."

She muttered something beneath her breath, slammed the door and returned to the driver's seat. The desk clerk was still watching, and Daniel had no doubt he'd made note of the license plate number. The powers that be were already on their trail, and Daniel wasn't quite ready to deal with them. Not until he had a better idea of the limits and extents of his new body.

He turned back, glancing at the dark sedan parked two doors down from their room. That car hadn't been there before. He didn't like the looks of it—the smoked windows, the heavy steel. That car's presence wasn't a coincidence.

The desk clerk had picked up the telephone. "Get a move on, Molloy," Daniel said.

She didn't wast her time arguing. Putting Jackson's car in gear, she took off, taking the corner at a dangerous speed, racing out into the night.

Daniel looked back. The door to the adjoining room opened, and he could see someone in a uniform that looked suspiciously familiar. Cole Slaughter. He glanced back at the sedan, trying to gauge whether it was powerful enough to catch up with them.

He stared at it, blinked and scrunched his nose absently.

The explosion sent Jackson's car skidding across the pavement. Suzanna swore as she tried to regain control, spinning the steering wheel and pumping the brakes desperately. They were heading sideways for a streetlight, and at their speed Daniel doubted they'd be able to avoid it.

But at the last minute she pulled out of the spin, straightened the wheels and took off into the night.

Leaving the anonymous sedan engulfed in flames.

Chapter Eight

"Oh, no." The voice beside her was hushed, literally disembodied, and yet distractingly solid. When Suzanna slammed her foot down on the accelerator, the car shot forward and she continued driving, hunched forward over the steering wheel like a bat out of hell.

An apt figure of speech. The flames shot into the sky behind them, sending ghoulish shadows across the road ahead. Suzanna yanked the wheel, turned into an alleyway and sped onward, away from the sight, the sound, the smell of the burning automobile.

She waited until they were out on the highway, away from the small town with its orange sky. "Was anyone in the car?" she asked quietly.

She didn't dare glance at the empty seat beside her. If she thought about it she'd be completely freaked out. Better to just be pragmatic about the whole thing. So the man beside her was invisible. Stranger things had been known to happen. She wasn't sure what, but they must have.

"I don't think so," the voice said after a moment's silence.

She couldn't resist. She glanced over at the empty seat, then swerved. "Do you have to wear your seat belt?" she demanded, thoroughly rattled.

The shoulder harness hung suspended in midair, the lap belt buckled across an invisible lap. "Habit," the voice said, and she heard the click of the seat belt releasing.

"Forget it. Do it up," she said, staring ahead of her. "I imagine you could get hurt if I managed to crash this sucker, and right now I'm feeling disturbed enough to do just that."

"Then slow down."

"Back seat driver," she muttered, nevertheless doing as he suggested. "What happened with that car? Was it another bomb?"

Silence for a moment. "Sorry, I was shaking my head. I don't think it was a bomb, any more than the other two were." He paused. "I think *I* did it."

"This is definitely weird," she muttered under her breath, not daring to look in his direction. "So how do you think you did it?"

"I don't know. Then again, I don't know how I got invisible, or how strong I am, or anything else. I'm learning as I go along. All I know is cars have exploded after I've stared at them."

"But every car you look at doesn't explode."

"No. There has to be more to it than that." She heard the faint creak of the seat, and she could only guess that he was shifting around, trying to get more comfortable. "We need to get away from everybody, so I can experiment."

"I don't know that anyone's going to be volunteering their car for the sake of science," she pointed out.

"This one will do nicely. The sooner we get rid of it the better."

"And how do you intend to replace it?"

Silence again. "Just drive," he muttered. "Head towards the mountains. Route 2A."

"Do you know where we're going?"

"Yes."

She waited for more clarification, but there was utter silence. She'd never realized how much she relied upon body language and facial expressions to read people. "All right," she said finally. "Mind if I turn on the radio? Sitting next to you gives me the creeps."

She startled him into laughing. It was a very sexy laugh, but then, she'd already known that about him. For an arrogant, starchy scientist, Dr. Daniel Crompton was extremely sexy. At least, as far as she was concerned, and she should have known better. That wry amusement in his voice traveled down her spine to lodge somewhere low in her belly, and she wanted to squirm.

"Go right ahead," he said. "I'll try not to be intrusive."

"That shouldn't be too much of a challenge," she shot back.

The radio didn't improve matters. Whoever was programming the music on the only station that came in clearly must have had an overload of hormones. The playlist was a hardheaded woman's nightmare. Chris Isaak was doing his werewolf impersonation on "Wicked Game," his voice sinuous and insinuating. That was followed by Marvin Gaye and "Sexual Healing," which had Suzanna shifting in the bucket seat and wishing to God she could see what Crompton's reaction to all this was.

The final song was Bruce Springsteen's "Fire." At that point Suzanna leaned over and turned the music off, thoroughly shaken. An unseen hand brushed hers, and the music came on again, slowly rocking, entirely suggestive.

"I want to hear it," he said.

"I don't."

"Tough. The irony is irresistible."

"Buy the CD then."

"I own it."

She turned to stare at him in surprise, seeing only her reflection in the passenger window. She turned back, cursing under her breath. "I saw your apartment, Dr. Crompton. You don't even own a CD player, and the only disk I saw was Neil Diamond's *Greatest Hits*. You live like a monk, and I can't say much for your taste in music."

Again that damnably sexy chuckle. "If you choose to believe that, go right ahead, Molloy."

"You're beginning to piss me off. Are you going to stay invisible, or will I be able to see you long enough to hit you?" she demanded.

"I have no idea. I changed back at eight this morning. Maybe in two minutes I'll be visible again."

She glanced at the digital clock on the dashboard. Seven fifty-eight. Bruce was finishing up, and Suzanna felt uncomfortably warm. Not that she wasn't used to it. From the first moment she'd been around Daniel Crompton she'd felt her temperature rise, and it wasn't just the furnacelike heat that emanated from his skin, seen and unseen. She had to face it, the man made her hot.

The radio station took pity on her, launching into a spiel for the kind of car she'd never be able to afford and wouldn't have wanted, anyway, and the seconds ticked away. "One minute to go," his disembodied voice murmured.

Then came an ad for laxatives, and Suzanna felt herself cool off. Until, God help her, a sultry male voice started discussing condoms.

The clock clicked to 8:00 p.m. Dr. Daniel Crompton remained invisible.

"So much for that theory," Suzanna said, hoping to drown out the conversation on latex sensitivity.

"Damn," he muttered. "I don't think I like the thought of remaining invisible."

She had a sudden, horrifying thought. "Are you wearing anything?"

She didn't have to see his grin to know it was there. "Interesting question, Molloy. What were you imagining?"

"How come I can't see your clothes? You aren't wearing the stuff that got dowsed with the slime, I know. Did you...I don't want to know."

She thought she'd already been unnerved enough, but the notion that he might be sitting next to her in the cozy front seat of the compact car, that long, elegant body of his undressed, was enough to make her want to drive off the road. Especially with the condom ad now over and Wilson Pickett coming on with "In the Midnight Hour."

"Don't panic, Molloy. Whatever I put on—or in—my body seems to disappear. If I just *hold* it, it seems to float through space. I'm still dressed."

"It could prove embarrassing if you were to suddenly rematerialize," she said in her coolest voice.

"For whom? You or me? Besides, I'm completely material now. You just can't see me. Much as you— damn." His voice suddenly sharpened, and there was no missing the thread of pain.

Suzanna slammed on the brakes, staring at the empty passenger seat. "What's wrong? Don't just sit there, Daniel, say something! Are you hurt? Are you . . ."

Before she could finish her sentence she saw the outline, vague, indistinct, slowly coming into focus. She'd forgotten how tall he was, and how he would crowd into the tiny seat of a compact car. She'd forgotten how long his legs were, too. He had an arm across his flat stomach, and as his face came into view there was no missing the expression of pain.

"Damn," he muttered again, closing his eyes.

"It hurts, Daniel?" she asked softly.

"Every time."

"How much?"

His eyes flew open, and he glared at her. "Enough to make your sadistic little soul happy, Molloy." He glanced down at his body. "I take it I'm visible again?"

"Can't you tell?"

"Not for certain. I look just a bit out of focus." He slid down in the seat with a weary sigh. "Three past eight."

"Maybe you'll stay invisible for longer and longer," she suggested. Having him beside her, suddenly visible, should have been reassuring. Instead, she found herself even more edgy.

"More likely the clocks aren't synchroized," he drawled.

"Why six to eight o'clock?"

"Why invisible?" he countered. "God only knows. Keep driving, Molloy. The sooner we get to my place, the sooner I can start working on some answers."

"Is that where we're going?"

"I have a cabin in the mountains," he said reluctantly. He rolled down the window, staring out into the night. "Fortunately no one knows about it. I keep it very private, and there's no way the people at Beebe can find us there."

"You think we'll be safe?"

"Maybe for a day or two. Then they'll find us, and who knows what'll happen."

"Oh, don't try to comfort me with reassuring lies," she said bitterly. "Just tell it like it is."

He glanced at her, and she found herself wishing that wry, clever smile was still invisible. It had far too potent an effect on her. "Are you worried, Molloy? I thought you were too tough to let a little thing like a megalomaniac megacorporation intent on murder get you upset."

"All in a day's work, Dr. Crompton," she shot back.

"You called me Daniel before."

"A slip of the tongue. I thought you were dying."

He nodded, amusement in his dark eyes. "I liked it," he said. "I'll let you know when I'm dying again."

SUZANNA MOLLOY WAS quite a woman. Whether Daniel wanted to admit it or not, there was no getting around the fact that she was tougher, smarter and far more determined than any woman he'd ever met. It wasn't that she met the challenge of having her companion literally disappear on her that was so impressive. It was the fact that it obviously scared her, scared her spitless, and yet she still managed to deal with it. Bravery without imagination was worthless. Resolution when you knew the consequences was far more honorable.

On top of that, she was the sexiest thing he'd ever seen. She still wasn't wearing a bra, a fact he'd been able to appreciate as he sat beside her, invisible. He would watch her long legs as she shifted gears, the play of her arms as she cornered, the soft swell of her breasts beneath the T-shirt. He could watch as her nipples hardened in response to the undeniably erotic music.

He was half tempted to see whether he could get away with touching her, but he didn't dare. Not this time. She was walking a tightrope of reaction. If he happened to brush against those luscious breasts, she'd probably scream and wreck the car.

He'd give her time. Not that that was a commodity they were particularly blessed with, but by the time they reached his cabin, out in the back of beyond, they'd probably have at least twenty-four hours of peace. Twenty-four hours for him to find some sort of answer as to what had happened to him.

And twenty-four hours to get her in bed.

He'd never set out to seduce a woman before. It was just one more novel experience, and he wondered idly whether the green slime had affected his libido, as well.

He didn't think so. He'd reacted to her in the moments in his lab, before the world and his life had exploded. Much as he would have liked to chalk it up to the aftereffects of the accident, he didn't think he could count on it. At best, having his life knocked sideways may have simply changed his priorities a bit. Before whoever had killed Jackson managed to catch up with them, he wanted to make sure he'd had a chance to see whether Suzanna ever stopped snarling long enough to purr.

"How are we doing for gas?" He kept his voice low, but she jumped, anyway.

"We'll need some."

"There's a truck stop up ahead. I've only stopped there once before, so people aren't likely to recognize me. We can get something to drink, maybe some food. It's going to be a long night."

"How far are we traveling?"

"You don't need to know. Suffice it to say we're not taking the most direct route. We'll be there by dawn."

"I'm not driving all night!" she protested.

"I am. I don't usually bother with much sleep. You can try to get some rest."

"For some reason, I don't feel particularly sleepy," she said with mock innocence.

He had the rash desire to lean forward and kiss her soft, cynical mouth. He would, but not now. "You've lived too staid a life, Molloy," he said calmly. "You're not used to life in the fast lane."

"In the fast lane on a back road?" she muttered.

"Maybe. There's the truck stop."

"Why is there a truck stop on a back road?"

"Beats me. You want to ask them?"

"No. I want a bathroom, I want a Diet Coke, and I want something to eat."

"They can provide all three."

He filled the tank while Suzanna disappeared inside the Quonset hut building. Jackson's credit card was lying in the glove compartment, and he used it without compunction. Jackson was beyond worrying about unpaid bills, and the good folks at Beebe might be a little slower in tracing it. At least it might slow them down a bit.

By the time he'd pulled up under the glare of the streetlights and gone in to find Suzanna, his sense of uneasiness was increasing. She was sitting at a booth, a huge greasy hamburger and french fries piled in front of her. He slid in opposite her, only to find the same noxious mass deposited in front of him.

"I'm not hungry," he told the slatternly waitress.

"You got a problem with the food, sonny?" the woman demanded, beefy arms akimbo.

"We're having a fight," Suzanna interrupted promptly, sliding the bottle of catsup across the table toward him. He caught it automatically. "Eat up, honey. I promise I won't bug you about Junior's report card."

He stared at her blankly, but apparently the waitress was satisfied. "Eat up," she said, in what was meant more as a threat than a suggestion, and disappeared back into the kitchen with a stately waddle.

"I don't eat meat," he said.

"Why not? Moral objections? Given that you're considered America's secret weapon, I find that just a tiny bit hypocritical," she said, picking up a french fry and popping it into her mouth.

"Where did you hear that?" he asked in a very quiet voice.

"My Uncle Vinnie. He knows everything."

"And what else did he tell you about me?"

She tore her attention away from her mound of french fries when she felt the sudden tension in the air. He'd already learned, however, that she wasn't easily intimidated. "He told me you were so brilliant they couldn't even measure your IQ. That no one knows what you've been working on, but it's big. Very big. Something that could change the future of the world. I don't like things like that, Dr. Crompton. I don't like the thought of one man having that much power.''

"I don't."

"All right. I don't like the thought of one man having that much knowledge or that much ability. Someone could control you. Everybody has some vulnerability. All they have to do is find yours, and you're putty in their hands.''

"I doubt it," he said, stretching out in the booth and taking the mug of coffee in his hands. It felt cool to the touch. "I don't tend to have recognizable weaknesses," he said, staring at one of the first weaknesses he'd ever noticed. "And why do you think we're running? If Osborn, Armstead or their goons catch up with us, I'm not sure what would happen. You'd think they'd want to keep me going, but they may have gotten some misleading information. They may think they have everything they need from me.''

"Do they?" she asked, forgetting about her french fries for the moment.

"No."

To his surprise she didn't ask him any more. She simply nodded, leaned back and concentrated on her food with a dedication that was single-minded and erotic.

He stared down at his own plate. Nothing short of starvation could get him to touch the hamburger, but the potatoes were smelling surprisingly good, and he needed something to cut the taste of the reheated coffee. "Tell me about Uncle Vinnie," he said, starting in on the fries.

"Nothing to tell. He's not really my uncle, he's my college roommate's uncle. He looks out for me."

"I'm a fairly obscure person. How would he have heard of me?"

She shrugged, managing an innocent smile. "Beats me."

His hand shot out and caught her wrist. He did it gently, afraid of his ability to hurt her, but there was no escape, and a flash of pure rage appeared in her warm brown eyes as she tried to jerk away. "Don't lie to me, Suzanna," he said quietly. "I've got top security clearance, and if someone has heard of me, it's someone who shouldn't have. Who and what is Uncle Vinnie?"

"You're hurting me."

"Answer me."

"He's just someone who looks out for me." He increased the pressure on her wrist, just slightly, and her face paled. She was lying to him, and he couldn't afford to let her do that. His life depended on it, perhaps hers as well, if he hadn't been wrong in trusting her. But he couldn't let her keep anything back.

"Who is he?" he asked one more time.

She wanted to keep resisting, he could see that. He could read the struggle, the furious acceptance. "His name is Vincenzo Dartaglia. He's retired from the restaurant business and he has certain contacts—"

"He's organized crime," Daniel corrected flatly. "What has he got to do with Beebe?"

"Nothing. He's just heard things, that's all. He warned me..." She took a deep, shaky breath.

"Warned you about what?"

"To keep away from you."

He stared at her for a long moment. "He was right," he said, releasing her wrist. "But you didn't listen."

"I'm not in the habit of listening to good advice," she said. She didn't rub her wrist, but he knew she wanted to. "He heard rumors about something going on at Beebe, and I decided to investigate. Obviously I got more than I bargained for."

"Obviously," he said quietly.

"I've learned one thing, though. You and Henry Osborn have a great deal in common."

He held himself very still. "What's that?"

"You both like hurting people when you want something."

"Osborn hurt you?"

She smiled at him. It was a cool, brittle upturning of her generous mouth, and he almost thought he could see the faint sheen of tears behind the glasses, in the depths of her defiant brown eyes. But Suzanna Molloy wasn't the kind of woman who'd ever cry. Who'd ever let a man like him make her cry.

"I'm tougher than that," she said. "He tried." She pushed her plate away. "I'll meet you at the car."

"Are you going to run away?"

She rose, and he noticed for the first time that she'd somehow found the time to put on a bra. It was the least he deserved as punishment. "No," she said. "I have a stake in this as well as you do. But, Crompton..." she leaned forward, smelling like flowers and french fries, utterly delicious.

"Yes?"

"You put your hands on me again and I'll cut your liver out."

He watched her saunter out into the parking lot, knowing his weren't the only appreciative male eyes marking her course. He could almost smile at her threat.

Almost—if he weren't so thoroughly disgusted with himself.

He told himself he'd had no choice. And it didn't matter. He'd never hurt a weaker, more vulnerable human being in his life. And the fact that he wanted her—needed her—made him even sicker.

Her wrist had been delicate beneath his encircling fingers, the bones and skin vulnerable. He thought about what he'd done to the locked door at Beebe, and he wanted to throw up.

What had Osborn done to her? He already had a score to settle with the man—Suzanna had just upped the ante. And it was only coincidental that when he smashed his fist into Osborn's fat, smiling face, he'd be aiming at his own, as well.

He'd hurt her, and he'd had no choice. And the damnable thing was, he might have to do it again.

Chapter Nine

Suzanna had already taken the passenger seat, fastened the belt around her and closed her eyes by the time Daniel joined her. Her wrist throbbed, and she wondered whether he'd actually hurt her, or if it was simply the heat from his skin. She didn't care. He'd used force on her, something she wouldn't easily forgive. So what if he was drop-dead gorgeous in a remote sort of way. She didn't need gorgeous. She needed tenderness, gentleness and decent behavior.

She turned her face toward the window, away from him, to hide the reluctant smile that curved her mouth. One of her worst problems, she'd learned long ago, was that she saw herself far too clearly. Life would be a great deal easier if she had some illusions about her own sweetness and gentleness. She'd left a number of her favorite T-shirts behind, including the one that read 51% Sweetheart—49% Bitch— Don't push it!'' She wished she was wearing it right now. It might remind her who she wanted to be when she grew up.

"You must be used to subservient females," she muttered.

"If I am, you're a refreshing change."

She bit her lip again, hoping he wouldn't notice. But Crompton was a damnably observant man.

"You couldn't be smiling, could you?" he asked in an astonished voice as he started down the two-lane highway.

She gave up, turning back to him. "What can I say? Life's too bizarre to be taken seriously."

He stared at her for a long moment, at the last minute turning his attention back to his driving before they ended up in a ditch. He drove in complete, utter silence for another five minutes, long enough for Suzanna to regret her remark, long enough for her to begin to drift off to sleep.

"I'm sorry I had to hurt you."

His voice was quiet, so low she should have missed it. He'd pitched it that way deliberately, and she knew he wasn't the sort of man who apologized. No more than he was the sort of man who made a habit of bullying people. He did what he had to do, and pity any poor creature who got in his way.

But she wasn't a poor creature; she could stand up to him. "Just don't do it again," she muttered.

She wasn't expecting it. He reached over and picked up her hand as it lay loosely in her lap. Her muscles tightened as she started to pull away, and his own grip grew stronger. She wasn't sure how a tug-of-war would end, but suddenly she didn't care. She let her hand lie in his for a moment, watching in fascination as he brought it to his mouth.

His lips were burning hot and dry as they pressed against the side of her wrist, where he'd crunched her bones together. The heat was like an electric current, shafting through her, and she turned, looking at him, wanting to move closer to that source of heat and strength.

But if he saw her reaction, he pretended he didn't. He set her hand back in her lap and kept his face turned into the night. "Get some sleep," he said. "We've got a long way to go."

She turned her face away again, uncertain what she wanted to say or do. She closed her eyes, feigning sleep, and within moments illusion became reality, as he drove through the endless darkness, the quiet drone of the car's engine lulling her to sleep.

She woke up several times during the night, turned to look at him, then drifted off again. The man wasn't human, she decided sleepily. No man could be so single-minded, so impervious to physical needs and discomfort. She slept again, dreaming erotic dreams—that his long, elegant hand skimmed her cheek, brushed against her breast, caught her hand in his once more and put it in his lap. And she didn't pull away in maidenly horror. He was hot for her, ready for her, as he drove through the night, and her hand on him was a kind of claiming.

When she finally surfaced from sleep, it was light outside. The radio was on, playing softly, something old and bluesy, and Suzanna shifted in her seat, a sleepy smile on her face.

And then she screamed.

"Damn!" he cursed, and the car swerved off the road, coming to a stop halfway up an embankment. "You scared the hell out of me. Did you have to scream?"

"Did you have to disappear again?" she shot back, furious, hoping he wouldn't notice that her hands were trembling.

"It wasn't up to me," his disembodied voice said, as the gearshift lever was put back into reverse, the steering wheel turned, and as the car started down the postdawn road again. "And I was right—this clock is three minutes fast."

She glanced down at the digital clock. It was almost seven. At least she'd missed close to an hour of Daniel's unnerving appearance. Or lack thereof. "Shouldn't I be driving?"

"The road's deserted. There aren't many people living out this way. If anyone looks too closely, they'll just assume this is a British import with the steering wheel on the opposite side."

"That's pretty farfetched."

"This entire situation is farfetched, but it's damnably real," Daniel replied. "We're not too far from my place now, and with luck we won't be passing anyone. Just let me concentrate on the driving, and we'll be there by eight."

"Just as well," she muttered. "I'd have a hard time following you otherwise."

Suzanna wasn't sure what she'd been expecting when they arrived at their mysterious, final destination almost an hour later. He'd called it a cabin in the woods, and she'd expected something rustic, with no amenities, just a reclaimed hunter's camp.

Either that, or another square box, as soulless and modern and characterless as Daniel's apartment.

The reality was astonishing.

Her companion stopped the car at the foot of a narrow, winding path, unfastening the seat belt and taking the keys. "We're here," his voice announced.

"Where?" she demanded, looking around her at the empty clearing, the tall, dark trees all around. They hadn't passed even a shack since she'd been awake, and she'd yet to see any sign of a building. "I'm not in the mood for a tent or a cave, Dr. Crompton."

She felt the air brush by her, warning her, and then his hand on her chin, cupping it, tilting her face upward, until she spotted the house.

It perched halfway up a cliff, and was made of glass and stone and wood, like some sort of new-age tree house. If he hadn't moved her head she would have missed it. As it was, the house blended in perfectly with the surroundings. "How do we get there?"

"We walk."

"I was afraid of that." She didn't bother to keep the mournful tone from her voice. He was still cupping her chin, and she could feel his long fingers against her jaw, delicate, strong, ridiculously erotic to her confused mind. And hot. "You can let go of me," she said caustically.

He did, quite promptly, and she had no idea whether there was any reluctance in him. One moment he was touching her, in what felt uncannily like a caress, in another he was gone.

The door opened and closed, and she could only assume he'd climbed out. She followed, grabbing her duffel bag as she went, unnerved to see his own canvas bag floating in the air. "I wonder," she said deliberately.

The canvas bag ahead of her stopped moving. "Wonder what?"

"If you took a cold shower, would the water sizzle?"

She heard him laugh, that damnably, sexy laugh. "I have no need of a cold shower, Molloy."

Depressing thought. "No, I suppose you don't," she said grimly, wondering if one would help her irrational state of longing.

"It wouldn't do any good," he added cryptically.

For a moment she considered his words. Would his body temperature withstand an icy bath? Or would his libido?

As far as she knew, the man didn't have a libido. And she had suddenly developed far too much of one. It must have come from having squashed it down for so long, she thought. She'd ignored any little trace of attraction she'd felt for the men she'd met during the last few years, and that squashed, downtrodden sexuality had decided to assert itself at the most damnably inconvenient of times.

She could fight it. She was tough. And fortunately Daniel Crompton had no sexual interest in her whatsoever. Right?

"Lead the way," she said wearily. "Unless you'd rather wait until you're visible again."

"What time is it?"

"You're wearing a watch."

"I can't see it."

"Oh." She glanced at her own. "Ten of eight."

"I don't want to wait. Move away from the car."

"Why?"

"A little experiment. Come over here."

She moved in the direction of his voice, trying to quell the uneasy feeling that washed over her. She walked to the edge of the narrow, snaking path that led up the cliff and stopped by the duffel bag that had recently floated through the air. "Is this far enough?" she asked in a deceptively even voice, bracing for the feel of his hands on her.

"Far enough." His voice was abstracted. She stood there, unmoving, listening to the wind rush through the tall pines overhead, bringing the scent of fall and resin to her nostrils. Nothing happened.

"Damn," Crompton muttered. "I can't do it."

"Can't do what?"

"Can't make the car explode. I was certain..."

The force of the explosion knocked her down. Where Jackson's little car had once stood, a fireball erupted, shooting flames into the sky. Suzanna lay on the ground, watching in horror, the heat enveloping her. She tried to rise, but something pushed her back down into the dirt, something unseen.

"Stay down," he ordered, but there was no panic in his voice. Merely a distant, sort of fascinated sound.

She did as he told her. Not that she had much choice. A hand rested between her shoulder blades, keeping her pressed to the earth, as the remnants of the automobile flamed furiously, burning out of control, and black smoke billowed toward the sky.

She closed her eyes for a moment and shuddered. When she opened them, the first thing she saw was his thigh. He was sitting cross-legged beside her, staring at the inferno, his hand still holding her down.

"It must be after eight o'clock," she muttered, struggling to sit up.

He released her, casting a cursory glance over her doubtless rumpled figure. "I figured it was. The cramps weren't quite as bad this time. Maybe I'm getting used to it."

"How did you do it?"

He nodded in the direction of the burning car. "You mean *that?* I'm not quite sure. I concentrated on it, but nothing happened. I think my nose itched, and I may have blinked a few times. I'll have to try to isolate it a little better. Find out whether it only works on cars, what causes the explosion, whether I can make other things—"

"I don't know if there'll be any more cars to spare," she said, her voice caustic. "How are we going to get out of here now that you've incinerated our only form of transportation?"

He had the grace to look momentarily abashed. "We couldn't go in Jackson's car, anyway. They'd be looking for it."

"You don't think anyone's going to notice the little bonfire we just had?"

"Not likely. We're in a very remote spot." He rose, and she looked up, way up the length of his jean-clad legs. God, it was a sin to be as good-looking as he was, she thought wearily.

"Let's hope so." She struggled to her feet, ready to slap away any helping hands. He didn't offer. He was already starting up the narrow winding path into the woods, and she had no choice but to follow.

She paused at the edge of the clearing, taking one last look at the charred remains of Jackson's car. Whatever had torched it had burned so hotly that even the frame had collapsed into the smoldering embers. It no longer even looked as if a car had been sitting there. The smoke had dissipated into the clear blue sky, and only the lingering smell remained. That and the blackened circle of earth.

She shivered again, despite the lingering warmth. And, hoisting her bag to her shoulder, she started after Daniel.

The woods were dark, overgrown, the path steep and slippery from early morning dew. Daniel forged onward, making no effort to wait for her, and Suzanna struggled to keep up, cursing underneath her breath. She'd just about given up hope of ever reaching the top, when Daniel stopped short, and she barreled into him, absorbing the solidity of his warm body, catching herself on his arms for a moment before she released him.

"Doesn't look like anyone's been here," he said in a meditative voice, still not moving out of her way.

She craned her neck around him, taking in their destination. It was like nothing she'd ever seen. A bizarre, crazy quilt of a cabin, it seemed cobbled together of wood and glass, iron and tile, a mishmash of found objects and odd humor. The door looked as if it belonged to an English castle, the windows on either side were crescents set in the thick walls, the roof was the greeny metallic of old copper. It looked like the Seven Dwarfs' cottage on drugs, and Suzanna stared at it, enchanted.

"This is yours?" she breathed, rapidly adjusting her opinion of the staid Dr. Daniel Crompton, as she'd had to so frequently in the last forty-eight hours.

"This is mine." His voice was neutral, exhibiting neither pride nor embarrassment.

"Where did you find it? Did you trade some crazed old hippie for it?"

He finally moved out of the way, advancing down the ornately patterned brick walkway and reaching up over the vastly high door to fetch a key. "No." He opened the door, standing aside with one of the first shows of gallantry she'd seen him exhibit, and ushered her in.

She fell in love. It was an extraordinary place, full of magic and mystery. The walls were of stained wood and covered with tapestries, quilted hangings, romantic watercolors and tempestuous oils. There were books everywhere—in cases lining every spare inch of wall, piled on the floor, underneath tables. The furniture itself was a blissful mismatch—a Danish modern oak table with three baronial-style chairs. A wide, overstuffed sofa covered in rumpled English cotton, a brass-and-steel table shaped like an elephant. It was a traditional decorator's nightmare. It was wonderful.

She turned back to glance at Daniel's oblique face. "Obviously you haven't owned this place for long," she said, touching a rubbed green velvet cushion with loving fingers.

"Why do you say that?" He closed the door behind them, and the light filtered in from the crescent windows, meeting the blaze of light from the window on the far wall, with its expansive view overlooking the forest below.

"Because you haven't had a chance to sanitize it yet." She picked up a book, caressed it and put it down again. It was, of all things, a Georgette Heyer regency. "You forget, I saw your apartment. If you had the chance, you'd strip this place bare and paint everything white."

"Why do you think I own this place?" It was a simple question, and she considered it.

"You probably bought it because it was so remote. You're not the most sociable of creatures, and you probably liked the fact that people would have a hard time bothering you here. Do you have a telephone?"

"No."

"Electricity? A television? Radio?"

"There's a generator, but no outside source of communication."

She nodded. She wanted to kick off her shoes and collapse into the huge, overstuffed sofa, taking the Heyer book with her. She restrained herself, but just barely. "You see. It proves my point. You own this place because you're an antisocial curmudgeon."

"If you say so." He moved ahead of her, opening up the windows, letting in the fresh forest breeze. There was still a tang of fire lingering in the air, a fact which brought their circumstances home all too sharply. "I'm not sure what there is for food. I don't tend to bother with it, but there'll be enough vitamin drink for both of us."

"Be still, my heart," Suzanna said. "Where do I sleep?"

For a moment there was silence, long enough that she turned to glance at him. "Like the five-thousand-pound gorilla, anywhere you please," he said lightly. "There's a loft upstairs with a bed, and there's the sofa. Take your pick."

"Where are you sleeping?"

Again that charged silence. And then he shrugged. "I told you, I don't sleep much." He dropped down onto the huge sofa, stretching his long legs out in front of him.

"I do," she said flatly. "And I need some coffee. You don't mind if I explore?"

"*Mi casa es su casa,*" he said, sliding down on the sofa and closing his eyes for a moment. She stared at him. For a man who didn't sleep much, he looked unutterably weary. He was used to life in a laboratory, not spending his time invisible, setting things on fire, running for his life and finding dead bodies. He probably wasn't used to having anyone else around, either. All things considered, she was probably lucky he hadn't set her on fire in a fit of pique.

She searched for the kitchen first. It was a small alcove off the living room, with open shelves filled with an odd assortment of staples—dried beans, brown rice and something that looked suspiciously like granola filled an assortment of mason jars. She found instant coffee and creamer, a tiny gas stove and a sink that after a moment or two of rusty shrieks gushed out clear mountain water.

She made a quick inventory. He was right, there wasn't much. Cans of soup, lots of them, thank heavens. Crackers, powdered milk, even powdered eggs. Could someone make a powdered-egg omelet? She had a feeling she was a long ways from her last quarter-pounder and fries.

She found a hand-thrown mug and filled it with the coffee. She'd always hated instant, but that morning, in that mysterious, enchanted little house, it tasted better than any cup made from freshly ground beans she'd ever had.

She took the step up into the living room to tell Crompton just that, only to find him stretched out on the sofa, sound asleep. He'd unbuttoned his shirt, and even from halfway across the room she could feel the heat in his body.

He'd damned well better not spontaneously combust, she thought grimly, staring at him. Apart from the fact that it would be a waste of a gorgeous male, she didn't want to have to deal with it. Though it seemed as if this particular gorgeous male was already going to waste.

There was a workroom off to the left of the living room, and for once Daniel's passion for order seemed to rule. Books lined the walls, stacked haphazardly, but the work surfaces were bare and pristine. More Georgette

Heyer. And science fiction, hardcovers, paperbacks, even a stack of comics. It was all very strange.

The walls were far from bare. They bore painted murals with strange, mythic images. There was nothing obviously sexual about them, and yet their sensuality seemed to reach out and entwine itself around her loins. How could the man concentrate in a room like this?

It had the same glorious view of the valley below. She opened the window, letting in the fresh cool breeze, and peered out, looking for any sign of habitation. There was none as far as she could tell. Daniel was right, they were remote and safe. At least for now.

It took her a while to find the narrow stairs up into the loft. It was a small room, with a king-size mattress at an angle on the floor. Light flooded in—a greeny, forest light—and the windows were covered with a filmy white cloth that looked like spiderwebs. The dresser was black-laquered Chinese, the rug was a kilim, the bed piled with antique quilts and laced pillows. Who had lived here, and why had they given it up to an ascetic grouch like Daniel Crompton?

When she came back down the stairs she paused, looking at the man sleeping so peacefully. His long black hair had come undone from the strip of material he'd used to tie it back, and it flowed around him. In repose he looked different. She would have thought he'd look younger, more vulnerable, but nothing could be farther from the truth. In sleep he looked every year of the thirty-four she knew him to be, and the elegant features of his handsome face looked intimidating. She moved closer, vaguely wondering how deeply he slept. She could feel the heat emanating from him as she approached.

He'd unbuttoned his shirt, and she could see his smooth, sleekly muscled chest beneath the denim shirt. She reached out a hand, to touch his forehead, to see if she could gauge his temperature, when his eyes flew open to meet hers.

"Look but don't touch," he said in an unbearably quiet voice.

She was mesmerized, by the darkness in his eyes, by the stillness in his face.

"Why?" she whispered.

"Because if you touch me, I'll take you. And I don't think you're ready for that."

The words shocked her into momentary silence. And then she fought back. "You're really arrogant, you know that, Dr. Crompton?"

He smiled then. A slow, devastatingly sexy smile that would have melted her bones if they weren't locked stiff with fury. "I know," he said. "And you're still not ready."

Chapter Ten

He couldn't have meant it. Suzanna leaned against the wooden counter in the tiny kitchen, staring into her mug of instant soup. Daniel Crompton was hardly the type to talk about taking her, like some romance hero bent on forced seduction. He was doing it to mock her.

But for once there had been no mockery in his dark, still eyes. They had been deadly serious, and she'd stumbled back from him, away from his heat, his intensity, away from temptation that was both a threat and a promise.

He'd risen from the overstuffed sofa, stretched, and he'd looked like a different man than the hidebound Dr. Crompton. His muscles moved sinuously beneath his skin, and he looked real, and dangerous, and far too human.

And Suzanna had run. She could hear him moving around in the living room, but she kept still, unwilling to face him for the moment as she concentrated on the watery soup. She was feeling warm herself, not uncomfortably so, and there was a faint tingling in her hands. Probably stress and exhaustion, she told herself. That would explain her idiot attraction to a man like Crompton, as well. Momentary insanity, caused by not enough sleep.

"Did you find something to eat?"

He stood in the doorway, filled it, and she wished she could tell him to button up his shirt again. She couldn't— the heat from his body filled the small kitchen, bathing her. "There's not much. What about you?" She was proud of the even tone of her voice.

"I can make my vitamin drink." He didn't move into the room, a fact for which she could only be grateful. It was a small kitchen. With him there beside her, it would be unbearably cramped. Dangerously so.

"You need something else. Aren't you human? Don't you have any physical needs?"

Wrong question. He just looked at her for a moment, and the temperature in the kitchen shot up another couple of notches. "There should be food in the freezer," he said. "I stocked it before I left last time, but I don't usually bother with it."

"You have a freezer?"

"A gas one. In the shed."

She managed a jaunty smile, hoping to cut the tension in the room. "Maybe I won't starve to death after all. The only thing that would make life complete is a bath."

"To the right of the living room."

"There's a bathroom, as well?"

"It's positively sybaritic."

She had to wait till he moved from the doorway. She trailed along behind him, through the living room, past a narrow door she hadn't noticed, then stopped short. "God," she breathed, "it's heaven."

The bathroom was larger than the kitchen. There was a stall shower made of azure tiles, a huge whirlpool tub encased in redwood, a stained-glass skylight letting in filtered rays. "The hot water's gas-fired, as well. You can sit in the tub for hours."

"Daniel, I love you," she muttered, brushing past his hot body. She turned around, a beatific smile on her face. "Who did you buy this place from? It's the most wonderful house I've ever seen in my life."

"I bought the land from a friend of mine. I own about four hundred acres, he owns the rest. That's why I figure we're relatively safe here. The surrounding forest is private land."

She had a sudden, unnerving thought. "You bought the land?"

"About five years ago."

"Then how did this house get here?" She didn't want to hear the answer. It would set all her preconceived notions awry.

"I built it."

"How did you get workmen out here, plumbers, electricians . . . ?"

"No," he corrected her. "I built it. Myself." He was watching her, gauging her reaction. "When it comes right down to it, construction, plumbing and the like is very mathematical. And I've always had a certain aptitude for math."

She just stared at him. She'd fallen in love with this strange, unexpected little house. That it was the creation of a man she already found far too disturbing to her senses, that it reflected his heart and soul and mind, was something she wasn't ready to accept.

"Enjoy your bath," he said, turning and leaving her there.

She heard the music as she lay in the tub, the cool, herb-scented water flowing around her. Somewhere in that outer room he had a stereo, and the music filled the place. Another anomaly. She would have thought he'd like free-form modern jazz, something arrhythmic, atonal, entirely intellectual.

Instead, it was the unmistakable sound of Lyle Lovett, singing something plaintive and soulful. Any man who listened to Lyle Lovett couldn't be all bad.

She didn't want to come out. She didn't want to look into his eyes again and see that cool, detached interest. He was far too tempting as it was.

When she emerged from the tub, she'd be calm, matter-of-fact, impervious to her own irrational streak. She'd make them something for dinner, and if things went as scheduled, she'd watch him disappear promptly at 6:00 p.m. She'd have an easier time with him if she didn't have to look at him, didn't have to keep her gaze from his thin, surprisingly erotic mouth. Didn't have to ignore his eyes, the set of his shoulders, the long, long legs and muscled torso.

Together they could figure out what they were going to do next. She certainly couldn't stay out here indefinitely, even if no one could find them. She'd go crazy.

Except that part of her wanted to drift. To lie in this cool tub of water, to float through this patchwork quilt of a house, to smell the piney air and breathe in the sunshine. She couldn't rid herself of the notion that she'd come home. And she wasn't ready to leave it quite yet.

When she finally rose from the tub, her body was still too warm. She combed her wet hair, slathered some cream on her skin and pulled on the clean clothes she'd brought with her. She surveyed her T-shirt with approval. It read If We Can Send One Man to the Moon, Why Can't We Send Them All? Perhaps Daniel would get the message. She only wished he would.

DANIEL MOVED ONTO the narrow balcony that hung out over the valley, and drank in the cool air. He let his shirt flap around him in the breeze as he leaned forward, gripping the railing. He couldn't imagine ever being cold again. Oddly enough, he wasn't particularly uncomfortable. It was a dry kind of heat, burning inside him, filling him with an edgy energy.

Suzanna was wandering around his house, a cup of instant coffee in her hand, a wary expression on her face. He didn't blame her. She didn't know what to make of him. She'd decided he had to be kidding when he told her he wanted her, and she'd pulled away from him, keeping her distance, treating it all as a joke.

It didn't feel like a joke. He wasn't used to wanting anything as badly as he wanted Suzanna Molloy. Right now it was all he could do to stand out in the afternoon light and concentrate on his erratic powers.

She'd spent an hour in his sybaritic bathroom, and when she'd emerged, fresh-faced, dressed in another defiant T-shirt, looking at him out of wary brown eyes as if he were a polar bear who'd wandered into town, it had taken all his concentration not to grab her.

He didn't consider for a moment that she might be wary of his freakish new powers. Molloy was made of sterner stuff than that. She was afraid of her own reaction to him. Something which pleased him enormously.

He heard her appear behind him on the narrow balcony. "What are you doing out here?" she asked quietly.

"A little scientific experimentation. I want to see whether I can set anything on fire."

She moved past him and leaned out over the railing. He allowed himself the luxury of admiring the lush curve of her hips in the faded denim. "Do you think that's wise?" she said. "I don't think a forest fire would solve anything."

"You're right. But from what I've observed so far, the heat is so strong, and so concentrated, that whatever catches on fire simply disintegrates before the blaze has a chance to spread. I want to see if I'm right."

"And if you're wrong?"

"Science is a far riskier business than most people realize. If you don't take chances, you never learn anything. See that tower through the trees? It's an old metal watchtower, from back in World War Two. It has no earthly use."

"So you're going to put it out of its misery?"

"I'm going to try." He leaned forward, concentrating on the wire structure, trying to remember how he'd managed to detonate the car. He stared, and nothing happened.

"Maybe it only works when you're invisible," she suggested after a long wait.

"No. Remember the parking lot outside my condo."

"What makes you think you're responsible?"

"An educated guess." He tried blinking a few times, but nothing happened. His nose itched, and he scrunched it.

There was no sound from that distance. Just yellow-white flames rocketing into the sky where the observation tower had once stood.

"Damn," Suzanna said softly.

At least he'd been right about one thing—nothing else caught. Within moments the fire was simply a gray plume of smoke, billowing skyward.

She turned to look at him. "Can you do anything besides metal?"

"I don't know. Pick something."

She peered over the balcony, then pointed to a clearly dead, huge white pine that lay in the midst of fallen trees. "Try that one."

The speed of it shocked him. He looked, he blinked, he scrunched, and the tree burst into flames. They watched in tense silence to see whether the fire would spread to the others, fallen timber, but it simply flamed out at the underside of the tree, leaving nothing but ash and charred fragments.

"Pretty neat trick, Dr. Crompton," Suzanna said in a cool voice. "Got any other little talents?"

He looked at her. She was trying to look blasé, but he could see the worry in her brown eyes behind the wire-rimmed glasses, see the faint anxiety in her soft mouth.

"I don't know," he said. "But I'm going to find out." His eyes narrowed. "You sure you're feeling all right?"

He knew it was cool out on the balcony. He didn't feel it, with his elevated body heat, but neither did she. She seemed perfectly comfortable wearing only a T-shirt.

"I'm feeling fine. Why shouldn't I be?"

"You got dowsed with the slime, as well. I can't figure out why you haven't been affected."

"Lucky me."

"Do me a favor. Pick an object, stare at it for a moment, blink and scrunch your nose."

"Why?"

"Indulge me."

"I feel like something out of 'Bewitched,'" she muttered, leaning forward. "That tree down there. To the left of what used to be the observation tower." She did as he'd ordered, concentrating. Nothing happened.

"Try it again."

"Trust me, Daniel, I don't have your ability to turn inanimate objects into cinders," she snapped. "You're the superman around here."

"I wish I could be sure."

"Of what?"

"Any number of things. That I was the only one affected. That it was only inanimate things."

She stared at him. "What do you mean?"

"Who's to say I can't incinerate another human being?"

He'd hoped saying it out loud would take some of the horror out of the notion. It only made it worse. He pushed away from the railing.

"I'll be in the lab, working on the slime. Maybe I can break it down enough to find some answers."

"An antidote?"

"If need be. Right now I think we're going to need all the advantages we can muster. I don't think the people at Beebe are going to forget about us."

"What makes you think they know I came with you?"

"They know," he said. And he walked away from her. While he could still make himself do it.

SHE DIDN'T MEAN to fall asleep. She was just going to lie down for a while on the surprisingly comfortable mattress upstairs, just close her eyes and feel the cool air across her skin. When she awoke, it was pitch-dark, and she could only hope it was after eight and she'd missed

Daniel's disappearance. She fumbled around for her glasses, then turned on the light beside the bed.

Her scream echoed through the eccentric little house. She heard Daniel, the pounding of his footsteps up the narrow flight of stairs, and while she'd managed to quiet her screams, she couldn't catch her breath. She felt her hands and face grow numb as she gasped for air, and the darkness was all around her, and she was going to die, she knew it, the green slime had simply taken longer to get to her, but it was going to kill her—

Hard hands caught her arms, shaking her. "Stop it," he said. "You're hyperventilating. Snap out of it!"

She bit back her choked protest. Some distant part of her brain told her that he'd be perfectly capable of slapping her if he thought she needed it. She took a deep, shuddering breath, trying to force her panic down.

"Good girl," he murmured, pulling her into his arms, against the fiery heat of his chest. He was wearing a T-shirt—she could feel the soft cotton beneath her clutching fingers, and beneath that the solid bone and muscle. It calmed her, as nothing else would.

"Don't call me *girl,*" she muttered, burying her face against his shoulder.

She could feel his smile. "Yes, ma'am. What happened? You're not the type of *woman* who has hysterics."

She pulled away reluctantly, staring up at him through her glasses. "I'm blind," she said simply.

For a moment he didn't move. "What do you mean by that? It's after eight—even I can see my reflection in the mirror."

"I told you, I'm blind. I turned on the light and everything's a complete blur."

"Blurred is better than blind," he said flatly. "Can you see some things better than others? When I'm invisible my body looks blurred to me, but everything else is in focus."

"I'm not invisible," she snapped.

"I know." He sounded just as rattled, which surprised her. "Just answer the question. Is everything fuzzy?"

"Yes."

She could see his outline as he sat on the mattress, watching her. "Describe it. In detail."

"It's the slime, I know it. I've been feeling hot all afternoon. Not a sweaty kind of heat, just a dry, tingling kind of warmth." She shivered. "When I lay down a few hours ago I could see perfectly. Now it feels as if my glasses are coated with Vaseline."

For a moment he didn't move. "Interesting," he murmured. And reaching out, he plucked her glasses off her face.

Everything focused, with a swiftness that was completely disorienting. She stared at him in the half-light, shocked. "This is impossible," she said in a hushed voice.

"Is it?"

"I've worn glasses since I was in the third grade. I can't see a thing without them."

"You can now."

She took her glasses from him and held them up. "Oh, my God," she said quietly.

"Welcome to the world of miracles," he drawled. He reached out and put his hand along the side of her neck in what felt alarmingly like a caress. She tried to jerk away, then stilled.

"That's better. I'm only trying to check your pulse," he said.

"Most people use the wrist."

"The carotid artery is a better indicator. Your pulse is racing."

"I've had a shock," she said, stubbornly ignoring the fact that his hand, straying inside the neck of her T-shirt, was doubtless responsible for at least part of her condition.

"Your skin is warm. Not as warm as mine, but warmer than it was," he observed in a detached voice. "Let me listen to your heart." He moved to press his head against her breasts, but this time she'd had enough. She jumped off the bed and skittered away from him.

"My heart's just fine, thank you," she said.

"I wonder why it took so long for it to affect you," Daniel murmured, suddenly analytical. "It's been more than forty-eight hours since the lab explosion, and I started being affected almost immediately."

"Probably because I didn't take a bath in the stuff," she said crossly. "You got the full brunt of it. I only had a little on my hands."

He looked at her, an arrested expression on his face. "I keep forgetting you have a mind."

"Do you really?" she said acidly. "I guess it's my blond bimbo looks."

"No," he said frankly. "But you *are* distracting."

She wasn't sure how she wanted to respond to that, so she avoided it, getting back to more important matters. "Did you learn anything about the slime?"

"Not yet. You can't rush these things."

"I thought we didn't have much time."

She was trying to rile him. She failed. "You have a point. I'm going back to work." He rose, and she got a good look at the T-shirt he was wearing. "Eat right, exercise, die anyway," it said. Hardly reassuring.

"What about dinner?"

"I'll make myself a vitamin drink."

"No, you won't. I'll make us something."

A wry smile curved his mouth. "You're feeling domestic, Molloy? I wouldn't have thought it of you."

"I'm feeling hungry," she corrected him. "And you need solid food, not vitamin drink. I want you to be in top physical condition."

His smile widened. "Any particular reason?"

"I'd like us to survive."

He touched her again. A brief, tender caress on the side of her face, a whisper of a stroke before he dropped his hand again. "We will, Molloy. I promise you."

She made him pasta, with every kind of vegetable she could find thrown into the sauce. He barely noticed her when she brought a tray into the lab, which was no longer the spotless operating room it had once seemed. Paraphernalia was strewn over the counters, and she shoved a pile of papers out of the way and dumped the tray down.

"Eat," she said.

"Eventually." He didn't move from the microscope.

"Eat," she repeated firmly. "I'm going to stay here and bug you until you do."

He lifted his head, focusing on her as if he'd forgotten her very existence until now. He probably had, she thought wryly.

He glanced at the overfilled plate and sniffed warily. "What's in it?"

"Broccoli, egg, green peppers, onions, mushrooms, pea pods and cheese."

"No beef?"

"There is no beef. Not unless I go out and rustle a cow myself," she said grumpily.

"Good." He hunched one hip onto a stool and took a forkful. He ate half the plate, slowly, methodically, and then looked up at her with dawning surprise. "It's good," he said.

"Of course it's good. I know how to cook. You just don't know how to eat," she grumbled.

He didn't take offense. "Good point," he said, rededicating himself to his dinner. He finished it, ate the garlic bread and then looked up hopefully. "Dessert?"

"I thought you didn't care about food."

"You're having an insidious effect on me." He rose, moving toward her, and it was all she could do not to back away from him. She'd been feeling warmer, but his heat still far outstripped hers. "Dessert?"

"I'll bring it in," she said in a resigned voice. "What about coffee? Or are you going to insist on some godawful herb tea?"

"Coffee," he muttered, considering it. "With caffeine. Lots of it." He turned and went back to the microscope, dismissing her presence.

She was half tempted to take the tray and slam it over his head. Who did he think she was—his maid?

Then again, she didn't necessarily want his presence. As long as he was immured in his lab she could ignore him. Or, at least, make a damned good stab at it.

He didn't look up when she brought the coffee and brownies in, and she left. He probably wouldn't notice cold coffee, she thought, stuffing her fourth brownie into her mouth. She stepped out onto the balcony, letting the cool air rush over her. The moon was bright overhead, almost full, and she could see a ring of frost around it. It was a cold night. And she could barely feel a chill.

She thought about the man behind the closed door, his erratic powers and the uncanny effect he had on her. She was in trouble—in very deep trouble—since the moment she'd first snuck into Beebe headquarters in search of the elusive Dr. Crompton.

The sooner this whole mess was resolved, the better for her heart and mind.

Because she was realizing, despite her best efforts, she'd done more than fall in love with the man's house. She'd begun falling in love with the man himself, and there was no future for a girl reporter and America's secret weapon. Particularly when he turned into a downside version of a superhero.

Chapter Eleven

Daniel rubbed a weary hand across his eyes. He was getting nowhere. Each time he thought he was on the verge of isolating the components of the slime, the solution escaped him. He'd been working for hours, stopping only long enough to wander into the darkened kitchen and get himself more brownies and coffee. He'd eaten half a pan of the brownies—he'd never realized he had a sweet tooth. He hadn't paid much attention to the coffee, but at least it had kept him going.

Until now. He glanced at his watch. It was quarter past five in the morning. He had forty-five minutes before he vanished again. He had a hard time working when he was invisible. The blurred outline of his hands distracted him as he worked at the microscope, and he'd jabbed himself in the eye more than once when he'd miscalculated.

Suzanna had disappeared hours ago, and he could only assume she was in the loft, asleep. Lying there, probably wearing nothing more than a T-shirt, her warm body soft and relaxed in sleep. He wondered what would happen if he kissed her. Closing the lab door silently behind him, he started upstairs to find out.

He stopped halfway up the narrow flight and turned, instinct calling to him. The door was open to the narrow balcony, and he could see her out there, bathed in moonlight, hands clutching the railing. And he realized with shock that there was a light snow falling.

He was wrong about the T-shirt. She was wearing a short, silky kind of nightgown, the kind he'd seen in a Victoria's Secret catalog he'd once perused, for scientific purposes, of course. It clung to her curves in a caress, and he wanted to follow those lush curves with his hand.

He came out on the balcony behind her. "It's snowing."

She didn't turn. She must have known he was there. Snow was drifting down onto her bare shoulders, lingering for a moment, then melting. "I had a dream about the man we found in the stairwell."

"Jackson," Daniel supplied. He moved closer, trying to warm her with his heat. She was cold, he could see it in the faint blue color to her soft lips, he could see it in the hardness of her nipples against the silk. He wanted her nipples hard. But he wanted to be the one who made them that way, with his mouth.

"It was an awful way to die."

"I'm not sure if there are any good ways."

She turned and looked at him, sorrow in her healed eyes. "Who do you think killed him? And why? Was it the same person who tried to blow up your lab?"

"I think Jackson was responsible for that. And I don't know why he was killed. Maybe he knew too much. Maybe he was trying to double-cross them. Maybe he'd just outlived his usefulness."

"It sounds like a James Bond novel."

He shrugged, moving closer. She was shivering; he was hot. She'd made a joke about a cold shower sizzling on his skin. He was surprised the snow didn't disappear in a cloud of vapor when it landed on his arms. "It's not a novel," he said. "Unfortunately it's real."

"Yes," she said, "it's real." Suddenly she rubbed her arms. "I'm cold," she added, surprised.

"Let me warm you." He pulled her into his arms, and after a momentary resistance she let him. The tremors that racked her body increased, and he scooped her up effortlessly, carrying her back into the living room and sliding the door shut behind him.

"Damn," he muttered beneath his breath. "I didn't get the heat going."

"That's all right," she murmured sleepily. "You're very warm."

He glanced down at her. He was more than warm, he was hot—for her. "All right," he said, moving to the huge old sofa, sinking down and bringing her with him. She was still shaking from the cold, and perhaps something else as well, and if he were a decent, honorable man he'd set her down and find her a quilt, wrap her up and leave her be.

He didn't feel the slightest bit decent, or honorable. He sat back, cradled her against him and caught her chin in his hand.

She stared at him out of those newly focused eyes, wary, waiting. But she didn't move when he put his mouth against hers, slowly, deliberately, his lips on hers. Her mouth was cold, and he warmed it. Her lips were dry, and he moistened them. He pressed his thumb against her jaw gently, and her mouth opened beneath his, so that he could taste her, and he heard a quiet little sigh, a moan of pleasure that could have come from her, or from him.

Her body warmed, softened, flowed against his. She lay curled in his lap, her hands clutching his shoulders, as he kissed her, kissed her until he was ready to go up in smoke, breathless, mindless, crazy with the heat and the need. She was soft and sleepy against him, and her tongue met his, shyly, with a touch of eagerness that just about destroyed him. He broke away, trailing slow, hungry kisses down the slender column of her neck, and she arched against him as his hand closed down over one breast.

It fitted his hand perfectly. Cool through the silky material, it warmed, swelled against him, and he wanted to taste her there, too.

There were buttons, damnable tiny pearl buttons down the front of the nightgown. He ignored them, sliding the thin straps down over her arms, baring her small, perfect breasts. And then he froze.

"Did I do that to you?" he demanded, pulling away.

The mood was shattered. Her eyes, dreamily half-closed, now shot open. Color flooded her face, and she yanked the nightgown up, backing away from him on the wide sofa. "Do what?" she managed to choke out.

"The bruises. On your breast."

She tugged the gown around her, a wasted effort, given the skimpiness of the thing. "No."

"Then who did?" A sudden, daunting thought entered his mind. He'd never for one moment considered that she might be involved with someone. The livid bruises on her breast might have been gladly received, the by-product of a little rough sex.

"Go away," she said, curling up in a little ball, turning her face away from him, into the sofa cushion.

He put his hand on her shoulder, felt her coolness, and he turned her, careful to temper his strength, refusing to let her hide from him. "Who did it?"

He could see by the expression in her eyes that it had come from no demanding lover. "Osborn," she said finally. "In the hospital room, when I was pretending to be unconscious."

The fury that swept over him was so strong, so powerful that he thought he might explode with the force and heat of it. He wanted to smash his fist into Osborn's fat, unctuous face. He wanted to storm and rage and kill.

The emotions startled him. He wasn't used to them, to the need for revenge, the fierce protectiveness, any more than he was used to the overwhelming lust he felt for the woman curled up in the sofa, her face hidden from him. Combined with an odd, soul-shattering tenderness.

He took a step away from the sofa, trying to govern his anger. "There are advantages to this," he managed to say in a deceptively cool voice.

She lifted her head to look at him, startled. Her cheeks were still flame red, but her mouth was soft, slightly swollen from his kisses, and he wished to God he wasn't still hard. That he could simply walk away from her, concentrating on his anger.

"What do you mean?" Her voice was quiet, wary.

He leaned against a bookcase. "I'll get a chance to see whether I can turn a man to cinders as quickly as I can a car."

She thought he was kidding. She managed a weak chuckle. "If Osborn holds still long enough for you to experiment."

"I'll make sure he does."

Something in his grim tone penetrated her self-consciousness, and she looked at him. "No, Daniel. I won't let you kill another human being. You're too civilized. It would end up destroying you."

"I'm not nearly as civilized as you think. I never have been. You've made any number of assumptions about me, and most of them have been wrong."

She glanced around her. "I was wrong about the house," she admitted. "But I'm not wrong about you. By nature you're cold, methodical, controlled. You're not a man ruled by his passions...."

He'd hauled her from the sofa before she had time to finish, pulling her up tight against him, her breasts pressed against his chest, her hips against his unmistakable erection. "If you think I'm cold, Suzanna," he said in a quiet, dangerous voice, "then you're forgetting what my hands feel like when they touch you. If you think I'm methodical or controlled, then you haven't been paying attention. And if you think I'm not ruled by my passions..." He kissed her then, hard, his hand threading through her hair to hold her head still, his mouth wet and hungry on hers, giving her no chance to evade him.

She didn't want to. With a little whimper of passion, she threaded her arms around his neck, arching into his embrace. He lifted her against him, and her long legs wrapped around him. Together they tumbled back onto the sofa, and her hands were sliding up under his T-shirt, cool, arousing, as her mouth answered his, and he was ready—

The first cramp hit him with the force of a blow to the stomach. He fell back, away from her, as if he'd been shocked. He willed the damned pain to stop; but it didn't—it washed over him, and he knew what was happening, and there wasn't a thing he could do to stop it. He shuddered, and there was a flash of bone-chilling cold sweeping over him, and his jaw locked in a grimace of pain before he shut his eyes, trying to ride that pain.

When he opened them again, Suzanna was across the room, white-faced. He looked down and saw the too-familair fuzzy outline.

He'd vanished again.

SUZANNA WANTED TO SCREAM and cry. She felt buffeted by emotions, feelings she hadn't experienced in years, if ever. Her body was hot, aroused, exquisitely sensitive, her mouth tender. And the damned man had the gall to disappear.

She had no idea where he was. Her own heart was beating too wildly, her own breath coming too rapidly, for her to hear his. She whirled around, heading for the stairs, stalking.

An unseen hand caught her wrist, halting her abruptly. She could feel the tensile strength in his fingers, and she remembered how easily those fingers had turned the metal lock to powder back at Beebe headquarters. He could do the same to her bones.

But he wouldn't. Despite the danger she had seen in his eyes, despite his insistence that he was far from civilized, she knew he wouldn't hurt her. "Let go of me, Daniel," she said in a very quiet voice.

His fingers encircled her wrist, his thumb stroking the pale, blue-veined pulse. She could see the movement of her skin beneath his touch, but she couldn't see his hand.

And then he let her go. She sensed him moving across the room, away from her, but he had a gift for silence, something that was particularly frustrating. "I'm going to go for a walk." His voice came from over by the door. "I'll be back at eight."

"You don't need to go," she found herself saying.

"Yes, I do." There was no missing the suppressed violence in his voice. The door slammed behind him, and she was alone, bitterly alone in the cold house.

She missed him. Missed the heat of his body, the strength in his arms. Missed his mouth. She'd been ready to let him strip off her clothes and take her, right there and then, on that overstuffed sofa that was almost as wide as a bed. While she should be thanking her lucky stars that fate had intervened, she found instead that she was merely shaking with frustrated reaction.

She took a fast shower, a hot one, to warm her chilled skin. It wasn't until she was pulling on a T-shirt that the obvious hit her.

Daniel Crompton wanted her. Wanted her quite badly, possibly as much as she wanted him. There was no disguising the passion in his mouth, the tension in his hands, the state of his arousal.

She sat down on the mattress, stunned. She could come up with all sorts of reasons why this realization should be disastrous. It was probably just a case of abstinence making the heart grow fonder. He probably had a bevy of willing females, back in Santa Cristina.

Maybe it was the danger that had caused his libido to react, making him reach for the nearest, the only female. Maybe he was the kind of man who simply had to make a pass at every woman.

Or maybe, just maybe, he was as drawn to her as she was to him. For whatever mysterious reason, no matter how impractical it might seem, there was something between them, something dark and dangerous, something bright and triumphant, something that went beyond petty misunderstandings or even the fate of the world.

She moved to the window, looking out into the morning light. It was cool and overcast, and she could see the blackened leaves that had been hit by the heavy frost. How long would he be gone? And what was he planning to do when he came back? Pretend it never happened?

Or finish what he started?

And she didn't know which possibility frightened her more.

IN THE END, it didn't matter. Daniel didn't return at eight o'clock. By nine o'clock Suzanna began to worry. By eleven she was furious. By twelve she was terrified. By one she went in search of him.

There was a light rain falling, more of a mist than an actual cloudburst. She followed the path, deeper into the woods, all the time fighting the questions that hurtled themselves at her head. What if he'd stayed invisible this time? What if Osborn and his crew had caught him? What if he'd decided he'd do better on his own, and he'd abandoned her?

She kept climbing, as the rain started soaking into her T-shirt, chilling her to the bone. She couldn't stand to go back to that cabin alone, not knowing what had happened to him.

In the distance she thought she caught a faint whiff of smoke, and she felt a sudden foreboding. She began to hurry, scrambling her way upward as the path steepened, sliding in the mud and scraping her arm, grabbing hold of old roots to haul herself up toward the ridge.

When she finally reached the clearing, she paused, momentarily stunned by the glory of the view.

And then she was equally stunned by the sight of Daniel, sitting cross-legged on the wet ground, completely visible. He didn't seem aware of her approach. He was busy staring at a row of several piles of refuse, brush and twigs and the like, and as she watched he set each one aflame.

Suzanna scrambled to her feet, seething. He glanced at her over his shoulder, then turned back to his little experiment, dismissing her as easily as he'd dismissed her this morning.

She walked over to him and stood directly behind him, wondering how she could hurt him. She was looking around, trying to find something to hit him with, when he leaned back against her legs, his head against her thighs, the warmth shooting through her like an electric current.

She reached down. His long black hair hung wet and loose on his shoulders, and she sifted her fingers through the silky length. And yanked, as hard as she could.

He let out a truly satisfying shriek of pain, leaping away from her. He ended up crouched on the ground, staring at her, shock and affronted dignity warring for control.

"What the hell did you do that for?" he demanded. "That hurt."

"You've been gone for hours," she said coolly. "I was afraid something had happened to you."

"Something did happen to me. A crazy woman tried to pull my hair out." He glared at her. "I don't understand what your problem is. I told you I was going for a walk."

"You left the house at six o'clock this morning. That was more than seven hours ago. I was afraid you might have fallen off a cliff."

"It probably wouldn't have hurt as much," he said, rubbing his scalp. "As a matter of fact, I was working. I tend to forget about time when I'm involved in something."

"Do tell," she said acidly. "And what have you discovered?"

To her increased discomfort he suddenly smiled at her. "Any number of things. I found I could regulate the area in which I direct the flames, and the intensity, as well. I can scorch something, or turn it to ashes. It's all a matter of control. I also checked the limits of my strength. I could push over that tree over there," he nodded in the direction of a good-sized pine tree that lay on its side in the mud, its roots brutally exposed, "but I couldn't lift it. My vision is the same—no x-ray capabilities, and I'm not—" he glared at her again "—impervious to pain. I don't think I quite qualify as a superman. My major talent seems to be reducing things to cinders."

"Okay, you can be Cinderman," she said. "It has a nice ring. I bet the *National Enquirer* will love it."

"Don't even think it."

She was finding an even more satisfying revenge than yanking at his hair. "They pay quite well, I hear. Especially if you've got something unique, and you, my dear Daniel, are definitely tabloid material. It's too bad we can't throw in a Cinderman diet and tryst with Princess Di, but even so, I imagine we can drum up a fair amount of interest. I could even put my story out for auction. I could be set for life."

She'd gone too far. The tension in his shoulders relaxed slightly, and he rose slowly and gracefully, the rain beating down around them on the high plateau overlooking the forest.

"You may not *have* a life," he said. "Not if Osborn and his pals have their way."

"Why? Why should they want to kill you, and me, as well? Why did they murder that man in the stairwell? And don't give me that James Bond crap again. I want to know exactly what is going on."

He considered it for a moment, watching her, and she half held her breath, waiting for another lie, another denial. Instead he came toward her, taking her hand in his and leading her back toward the steep path.

"I want answers," she said, trying to hold back.

She might just as well have tried to stop a raging bull. Daniel kept moving, and his grip on Suzanna never loosened, so that she was forced along after him, skidding a bit in the mud.

"You'll get your answers," he said, starting down the steepest part. "But first I need a hot shower, some coffee and something to eat."

"You can make your vitamin drink."

He glanced back at her, and there was that damnable, seductive sweetess in his smile. "I think I've developed a taste for brownies," he said. "Among other things. Come along, Suzanna."

Following him down the narrow, winding path gave her plenty of time to think of revenge. Never once did he let go of her hand; even when she slid and skidded into him, he absorbed the blow with calm determination. She could always push him off the balcony, she thought. Or maybe get him to try his incendiary powers on a propane tank.

The house loomed up out of the mist, sooner than she would have thought. "Wait a minute," he said, finally releasing her hand, not noticing that she did her best to snatch it to her in affronted dignity. "Stay put."

He advanced on the house silently, doing a swift surveillance. He disappeared behind it, then came back. "I don't think anyone's been here," he said.

"If you thought someone might show up, why did you leave me here alone?" she demanded.

"Oh, I knew you were more than a match for any of Armstead's little army who might happen to show up. You could pull their hair," he said cheerfully.

The balcony, she thought, fuming, brushing past him as she entered the house.

It was damp and chilly inside, and Suzanna shivered. "I'm going to change my clothes."

The moment he closed the door behind him the temperature rose, as if someone had just turned on the heat. "Some coffee would be nice, to go with the brownies," he said.

She just looked at him. "Learn to cook."

Lord, the man shouldn't have a smile like that! Just when he was already driving her crazy. "You can teach me," he said.

"Daniel . . ." she called after him.

He paused, looking back at her. "What?"

She didn't know what she wanted. Him to touch her, him to kiss her, him to disappear back into his lab or the ether or wherever so he wouldn't be so infuriating, so distracting, so irresistible.

"Don't take all the hot water," she said.

You could take a shower with me, his mind said, so clearly that she thought she heard his voice speak the words.

"All right," he agreed after a moment.

She watched him go, shaken. It had been her imagination. The result of God knew what kind of stress. She couldn't have heard his thoughts—it simply wasn't possible.

But it wasn't possible that her twenty-year nearsightedness had suddenly been cured, and it wasn't possible that Daniel Crompton could set things on fire and turn invisible from six to eight every morning and evening and have superhuman strength. Nevertheless that was exactly what had happened so far.

And now she could read his mind. It was a gift she could have done without, and if it were up to her she'd shut it off.

But it wasn't necessarily up to her, any more than Daniel could control whether he turned invisible or not. She could only hope he'd figure out an antidote to the green goop fast. Before she developed any more unnerving talents.

Chapter Twelve

Suzanna stripped off her rain-sodden clothes, pulled on fresh ones and sat cross-legged on the futon mattress. She didn't want to look at Crompton, didn't want to give herself the opportunity to read his mind. Too much had happened in the last forty-eight hours or so, and she wasn't quite ready to deal with all the ramifications. She didn't want to be able to look into Crompton's cool, dark eyes and see what he thought of her. There were some things better left unknown.

There were piles of books and newspapers in the bedroom as well as every other square inch of the house, and she grabbed for the first thing she could reach. To her amazement she found it was a book on the Spanish riding school in Austria, an odd choice, but in keeping with the catholic nature of his library. He seemed to have a book on almost every subject, and his interests were absurdly varied. She'd seen science fiction, books on car mechanics, financial guides, what seemed to be the complete works of Georgette Heyer and Jane Austen, the history of costume, mixed in with books on scientific subjects so arcane that even she, with her Ph.D., was appalled.

She'd never been particularly interested in horses, but as she heard Daniel leave that absurdly luxurious bathroom she opened the book and immersed herself in the text, determined not to let an errant thought, either hers or his, stray into her consciousness.

"I saved enough hot water for you." His voice floated over the balcony of the loft bedroom.

She didn't answer, concentrating instead on the fine points of dressage. Until she heard his voice at the bottom of the stairs.

"Suzanna?"

She didn't want him coming up there. She didn't want to be in the same small area, looking at him, remembering what had happened in the predawn, remembering the feel and the touch and the taste of him. "I'm fine," she called back. "I'll take a shower in a little while."

Silence, and she held her breath, staring fixedly at the words as they swam in front of her. "I'll be in the lab then," he said. "I'm not likely to surface until you come and get me."

"Fine," she said airily.

Come and get me, his mind echoed in hers, and she pushed her face closer to the book, trying to push his thoughts away. A moment later the door to the lab closed, and she breathed a sigh of relief, rolling onto her back, the book forgotten at her side.

There was a roof window above and the autumn dusk was already settling around the funny little cabin. She could see the massive pines overhead, swaying in the wind. Despite her dry clothes, she was still chilled, and she pulled the duvet around her, turning her face into the pillow, closing her eyes, closing her mind, shutting out the doubts and fears that had been plaguing her. She never thought she was the kind of woman who had doubts and fears. She was tough; she met challenges head-on.

But these recent challenges were too much for her. She wanted peace, she wanted comfort, Lord, she wanted someone to take care of her! An extremely odd notion, when she'd learned through her life that the only person she could rely on was herself.

She wanted to rely on Daniel Crompton. She wanted to know that she didn't have to watch her back, that he'd be watching for her. Just as she could watch out for him, as well.

She wanted a partnership, true love, happy ever after, all that stupid, preprogrammed, fairy-tale stuff that she'd resisted all her life. And she wanted it with Daniel Crompton.

She could hear him moving about in the lab. If she held herself very still, she could hear his thoughts bubbling around in his brilliant mind. He wasn't thinking about her, he was thinking about the green slime. A reassuring, disappointing realization, Suzanna thought with a wry grin.

And pulling the duvet over her head, she fell asleep.

FOR THE FIRST TIME in his life, Daniel was having trouble concentrating. As he hunched over the microscope, adjusting the field, he kept thinking about Suzanna. About the magnificent rage in her warm brown eyes, no longer fettered by glasses, the force in her hands as she'd yanked on his hair, the fury that had vibrated through her tall, gorgeous body.

He had looked at her out on that rain-swept ridge, at the rage and frustration in her face, and known that she loved him. He was still reeling from that knowledge.

She was fighting it—he knew that full well. She didn't want to fall in love, and he couldn't blame her. From what he'd observed, it was messy and inconvenient, distracting even the most disciplined mind from more important matters. Look what it was doing to him.

He lifted his head, stunned at the realization. Hell and damnation, he was not going to fall in love with Suzanna Molloy. She was beautiful, brilliant, cantankerous and an intrusion into his well-ordered life.

Except that his life had been far from well-ordered recently. Having his lab blown up, being covered with green slime, turning into—what had she called him? Cinderman?—had all been far from conventional. Falling in love would be the coup de grace, and he had every intention of fighting it tooth and nail.

That didn't mean he didn't revel in the fact that the mighty Suzanna Molloy had fallen. And he had every intention of taking advantage of that fact, as soon as she'd hold still enough for him to get her in bed.

He might even marry her. He'd never considered marriage, but having spent forty-eight hours with the cranky Ms. Molloy, he could see it would definitely have its advantages. He'd discovered an absolute craving for brownies. And for Suzanna Molloy.

He wondered idly how much convincing she was going to need. She was very, very bright—that was part of what drew him to her. He could simply state the obvious advantages of a union, and if she were as sensible as she was intelligent, she'd agree.

In his experience, women were seldom sensible. Even the best and the brightest of them, and Suzanna fitted or even transcended that category. She might be just as likely to throw his well-planned suggestion in his face.

He leaned back, staring out into the darkening sky. Maybe he'd simply have to seduce her into complying. It had certain appeal. If it hadn't been for the damned clock, he would already have accomplished just that, and there'd be no more arguments about who was going to sleep where.

Or maybe, just maybe, he was better off keeping his distance. Suzanna affected him as no other woman had. Enough so that he was sitting over his microscope, staring out into the twilight like a lovesick calf instead of working. He needed to concentrate. He needed to stop thinking about Suzanna. And the surest way to do that was either to get rid of her or to sleep with her.

If he was truly sensible he'd opt for the former.

But then, good sense had never been his forte. He'd spent his life following his intellect, his instinct, his inclination. And while this time those three things had parted company, he was going to go with instinct and inclination. He was going to make love to Suzanna Molloy so thoroughly that he wouldn't even need to think about her for days.

And then maybe he could solve the riddle of the mutated green slime, and just what it had done to him.

Six o'clock came with damnable regularity, one of the few constants in a world gone awry. He sat back when the first cramp hit him, cursing under his breath, tensing against the pain. It rippled through him, cold and blinding, and then he was gone.

He rose, furious with himself for wasting so much time when he could have been working. Of the hours since they'd been back at the house, he'd spent the vast majority dreaming about Suzanna's legs, wrapped around his back. And while there was nothing he wanted more than to go in search of her, to see just how limber those long, beautiful legs were, now wasn't the time to do it. Even if she couldn't see him, she could feel his touch, and he didn't think she was ready to do it with the Invisible Man.

What he needed was more brownies. He stepped out into the living room as quietly as he could, closing the door behind him. There was no sound from Suzanna, and he glanced up at the loft. A light was burning against the encroaching darkness, but he could hear the evenness of her breathing, the quiet steadiness of her heartbeat. She was asleep.

The brownies were gone. He considered heading upstairs after her, then changed his mind. Instead he threw himself down on the sofa, propping his head on his arms. He listened to the steady thump of her heartbeat, concentrating on it, feeling his own heart beat in rhythm with it. He let himself drift, then slide into the sleep he'd been resisting.

HE WOKE WITH A START, the darkness all around him, and then he heard the sound of the shower.

He lay on the sofa, imagining her in there, water sluicing down over her skin. He wanted to go in and lick the water off her.

Instead he waited for her, listening.

For once fate was kind to him. The door opened, and Suzanna stepped out, her eyes searching the living room warily. She was wearing nothing but a towel. A towel that was definitely too skimpy for her tall, wonderful body, and she clutched it to her like a lifeline as she tiptoed across the room, heading for the stairs. And then she stopped, startled, like a doe caught in the headlights of an oncoming car.

"Damn it, are you in here, Crompton?" she demanded furiously.

"Guilty."

Her face swiveled toward the sofa and the sound of his voice. "Close your eyes."

"You trust me?" The thought amused him.

"Enough to close your eyes if you say you have."

"I've closed my eyes," he said promptly, honestly.

The tension in her body lessened slightly, and she scampered across the room, towel trailing behind her, and raced up the stairs to the loft, and out of sight.

"Thank you for being a gentleman." Her stiff voice floated over the edge of the balcony.

"My pleasure," he murmured. "But to be perfectly fair, I ought to tell you I can see through my eyelids."

The book came sailing over the balcony, landing dangerously close to his head. He rolled out of the way in time, and he found himself grinning like an idiot. It was just as well she couldn't see him. She'd probably slap the smirk off his face.

"You know, Molloy, you're going to give Armstead's and Osborn's goons a run for their money when they show up here," he drawled. "You just need to improve your aim."

She leaned over the balcony, glaring. The T-shirt she'd pulled on read I Love My Attitude Problem, and her wet hair hung down like something out of a fairy tale. "At least I'll be able to see what I'm aiming at," she snapped back. And then there was a sudden, stunned expression on her face. "What makes you think they'll find us?"

"They will. It may take them a while, but they have resources at their disposal that effectively destroy any secrets we might hope to have. They're going to find us, Suzanna. And they're going to try to kill us."

Her face was already pale, but even in the shadowy light he could see the ashen color increase. "Why would they destroy America's secret weapon? Don't they have a use for you any more?"

"They've got two problems. One, they know that I'm not going to work for them any longer. As long as they left me alone, gave me plenty of money, then I was reasonably content. They would have gotten their hands on whatever I discovered in the long run, so they may as well foot the bill and let me work in comfort. And two, they don't realize that they don't have complete documentation of my work. If they did, they wouldn't risk harming even a hair on my head."

"What is it?"

He was getting a crick in his neck, staring up at her. "What is what?" he asked testily.

"What are you working on?"

"You've been trying to find that out ever since you snuck into my lab. I'm really not interested in playing Romeo and Juliet. Come down from your perch and I'll tell you."

She looked wary. "I'm not sure if I believe you."

"What have I got to lose? We may both be dead tomorrow. You might at least know what you're dying for."

"I have no intention of dying," she said, coming down the stairs, keeping her face averted from his general direction.

"Just as well," he said. "I have no intention of letting you get killed." At least, not if I can help it, he added to himself.

She paused at the bottom of the stairs, her head cocked to one side, as if she were listening. "And what if you can't help it?"

Her echoing of his thoughts unnerved him for a moment. "You forget," he said in a passable drawl. "I'm Cinderman. Able to leap tall buildings in a single bound. Faster than a speeding bullet, more powerful than a locomotive..."

"Not that I noticed," she said, edging her way over to the sofa. "You're strong, but I haven't noticed you being particularly fast. As for being able to leap tall buildings..."

"Don't be so literal." He started to move closer, slowly, silently, not wanting to scare her away. He wanted to be near her. To look at her, the high cheekbones, warm brown eyes, the erotic, touching vulnerability in her wide mouth. He wanted to see whether she was wearing a bra or not, he...

She crossed her arms across her chest, glaring at him. "You're still avoiding my questions, Crompton. What are you working on?"

He wasn't about to tell her it was something even more powerful than cold fusion. She wouldn't believe him, and the more she knew, the greater her danger. If she understood the details of bi-level molecular transfer, she'd be—

"You're crazy," she gasped. "There's no such thing as bi-level molecular transfer."

He gave up trying to sneak up on her. He crossed the room in three swift, noisy strides, clamping his hands down on her shoulders and swiveling her around to face him. Not that she could see him. Which was just as well. He'd probably only scare her if she could read his expression. "What did you say?"

There was no way she could miss the quiet menace in his voice but as usual, she didn't let it cow her. "I said, there's no such thing as bi-level molecular transfer. You know as I do that it's a fairy tale, a mad scientist's fantasy. The sort of thing that kept Merlin busy. It doesn't exist."

"It does."

He'd managed to shock her into silence. It was only temporary, of course. "Even you aren't that smart, Crompton," she said weakly, but he could see she believed.

"Why do you think they call me America's secret weapon? I've developed something so powerful, so legendary, that the world as we know it would be changed forever if it gets out."

"What do you mean, *if* it gets out?"

"The good folks at Beebe don't even realize what they've got under their nose. They think it's cold fusion, and they're willing to kill for it."

"Bi-level molecular transfer would make cold fusion seem as archaic as an A-bomb. But what about the practical applications? Surely you can't have gotten that far?" She still seemed stunned by the magnitude of his discovery. As she should be. He released her arms, and she sank down on the sofa.

"What good would it be without practical applications? Proven theory is all fine and good, but you have to be able to make it work."

"And you can make it work," she said in a hollow voice. "Exactly who are the folks at Beebe? You said they would have gotten their hands on it sooner or later, so you decided to work for them. Who are they? They're not organized crime, or Uncle Vinnie would know. Are they CIA? The government? What in God's name is Beebe Control Systems International?"

He considered walking away. She wouldn't be able to find him, make him answer questions he'd never answered before. Even if she could see him, she wouldn't be able to do that.

But the damnable thing was, he wanted to tell her. For the first time in his life, he wanted to talk to someone about the convoluted world he'd been living in.

"Beebe stands for BB. Big Brother. And that's exactly who supports and owns Beebe. You're wrong about organized crime. The board of BBCSI is composed of some of the most powerful people in the country. They've got Mafia, they've got four-star generals. FBI, CIA, the far right. All the most power-hungry, paranoid groups that make up this country's power elite."

"I thought the cold war was over."

"You thought wrong. At least, it's not over as far as these people are concerned. They're convinced the Russians are just biding their time, stockpiling weapons. They think the sooner they can nuke the Middle East out of existence, the better. They're looking for some nice clean way to gain control over the world, and then they can make their own rules."

"And you went along with that?" she demanded, obviously horrified.

He shrugged, but of course she couldn't see that. "I didn't pay much attention to who was paying the bills. The same kind of people are in charge, whether you work for the government or academia. You just learn to keep your secrets."

"Have they got yours?"

She could be a liar, he thought coolly, dispassionately. She could be a plant, a practiced actress hired by Osborn and his crew to ferret out his secrets. If he told her the truth, trusted her, he could be signing not only his death warrant, but the fate of the world, as well.

"I'm not a liar," she said. "You can trust me."

He considered it for a moment. And then deliberately made the first step. "They only have half of them. Jackson was copying my research during the last few months—I had a safety lock on the system that recorded every time security was breached, and who did it. But I kept a great deal of my research separately, with me."

"Where?"

He smiled, a wintry smile that she couldn't see. "On a CD disk. It looks like an audio disk instead of something for the computer. The only way you could tell it was a ROM disk was if you tried to play it on the stereo."

"Would it destroy the disk if you did that?"

"Why? Are you thinking of going back to my apartment and finding the rest of my research? The boys at Beebe are very eager to get their hands on it. You could be a very rich young woman, set for life. If they didn't decide to kill you, as well."

"Stuff it, Cinderman," Suzanna snapped. "I don't deserve that. And it's not necessarily the smartest thing you've ever done. It's got to be that Neil Diamond CD. Anyone with any brains would wonder what you'd be doing with something like that. Someone could break into your apartment, take it, and you'd be up a nasty creek without a paddle and they'd have the power to change the world, and probably not for the better.''

''Not really.''

She peered through the gathering darkness, but there was no way she could see him. He held very still, keeping his breathing quiet, not wanting to give away his presence. ''What do you mean by that?''

''I mean there's a crucial piece of the puzzle missing, both from my research in the computers back at Beebe and from the CD ROM.''

''And where is that piece of the puzzle?''

''In my brain.''

''Don't be ridiculous,'' she shot back. ''You can't rely on memory for something that important.''

''I can. I have a photographic memory. You'd be amazed at the stuff I have crammed into my brain.''

She rose, staring in the direction of his voice, and he wondered coolly whether now was the moment of truth. Whether she would tell him who and what she really was, and what she wanted from him. Had he been wrong to trust her?

''Damn you,'' she said in a low, furious voice. ''How dare you?''

''How dare I what?'' He was momentarily astonished.

''How dare you question who and what I am?'' she said, stalking toward him. ''I've let you drag me to the back end of beyond, do your disappearing act, lie to me, then treat me like you trust me, when all the time you've been standing there thinking I'm some kind of penny ante Mata Hari, out to steal your secrets and then cut your throat. If I could only see you, I'd be more than happy to..."

She walked right into him, and his hands came up to capture hers. Before he could think about what he was doing, he did what he'd been wanting to do. He pulled her into his arms and put his mouth on hers, silencing her.

She didn't fight, even though he could feel the rage and resistance in her body. She stood there in the circle of his arms, letting him kiss her, and she felt cool and still against his heat.

Her lack of response should have been a deterrent. It only increased his determination. He used his tongue, sliding along her lower lip, and she opened her mouth for him, reluctantly, and her arms moved up around his waist as she softened against him, absorbing his warmth, absorbing his need, until she was suddenly kissing him back. Her hands clutched at him tightly, and her heart was pounding fiercely against his.

He reached up and cupped her face, his fingers sliding into her shower-damp hair, and he pulled her away and stared down at her. "One question, Molloy," he said in a raspy voice, only slightly breathless.

She closed her eyes and became very still, waiting. "What is it?"

"How long have you been able to read my mind?"

Chapter Thirteen

Suzanna tore herself away from him. Her lips were hot, burning, from the feel of his mouth against hers. Her skin was on fire, itchy, and yet she only wanted the feel of his body against hers. Only the touch of his flesh would soothe her.

She turned her back on him, staring out into the gathering darkness. "I hate trying to talk to you when I can't see you."

"How long have you been able to read my mind?" The question came again, inexorable, and she knew there was no escaping it. She wasn't quite sure why she wanted to.

"I can't read your mind," she said. "I can hear thoughts. And it's only been since we came back from the ridge." She turned and looked back at the empty space where she assumed he was standing. "I don't like it."

"I can't say I'm any too crazy about it, either," he drawled. "What am I thinking about now?"

"If I could find you I'd slap you," she said. "You're thinking about my breasts again."

"That might just be a logical guess. Try again."

She closed her eyes for a moment, opening her mind. And then she shook her head. "It doesn't work."

"What do you mean?"

"I mean I don't seem to be able to control it. Errant thoughts filter through, when I least expect it, but if I try to reach out for your mind, I just get a blank. Let's face it, Mr. Spock I'm not. There's no Vulcan mind-meld for me."

"Maybe if you touched me."

"No, thank you," she said sharply. "It unnerves me enough as it is." She ran a hand through her damp hair, taking a deep breath. "What time is it?"

"I don't know. I can't see my watch."

She was cold. It seemed at times that the only way she would ever get warm was to be near him. And yet that was a danger far greater than anything she'd imagined so far. Freezing to death was a dreamy, painless way to go. Death by fire was terrifying.

And yet, like a moth, she was drawn to the flame. The heat of her possible destruction beckoned to her, and she didn't know how much longer she was going to be able to resist.

She heard his swift, pained intake of breath, and for a moment she didn't realize what it signified. He rematerialized slowly, fuzzily at first, and she forced herself to watch him.

"Is it getting worse?" she asked quietly.

He leaned back against the wall, taking deep breaths. His rumpled white shirt was unbuttoned, hanging loose around him. She'd felt that skin against her when he kissed her, wondered what he'd been wearing. Now she could see it, see his lean, muscled chest, the faded, tight jeans that clung to his long legs, his bare feet on the polished wood floor. His hair was tied back, his face looked severe, remote, and she wanted to cross the room and taste his mouth again, now that she could see it.

"Eight o'clock on the dot," he said, glancing at the thin gold watch he wore on one tanned wrist. He looked up at her, and there was a dark, haunted expression in his eyes. "I'm getting tired of this."

"Superpowers aren't all they're cracked up to be?" she said, deliberately keeping her distance, when she felt the pull, as strongly as a magnet on a piece of steel.

"What do you think, oh swami mind reader?" he countered.

"I like being able to see without my glasses."

He shrugged. "I imagine I could come in handy on a camping trip, if someone forgot the matches."

"I'd do well on television game shows."

"I could get a job moving pianos for a living."

She smiled. She couldn't help it. She didn't want to, but somehow the ludicrousness of the situation got to her. "We make a ridiculous pair," she said wryly.

The silence, the heat in the room, was palpable. "I wouldn't say that," he said. "Come here, Suzanna."

The wariness in her body flared into a moment of outright panic. It had been leading to this for a long time. Longer ago than the moment he'd come back to his lab and found her there. It had started with their very first confrontation, at one of Beebe's unctuous public relations efforts. She'd clashed with him then, and she thought he'd dismissed her with his typical scientific arrogance. She knew otherwise now. He remembered that first clash. He was remembering it now.

"Don't," she said, trying to shut it off.

"Come here, Suzanna."

It was her choice. It always had been. She stood by the balcony, and the chill of the autumn night radiated through the glass door, sinking into her bones. It was cold and dark and lonely there. And safe, but was it a safety worth the price?

She looked at him, trying to gauge how much he wanted her, and the longing was so strong, so fiery, it warmed her from across the room. I burn for you, his mind said, his eyes dark and haunted. And the choice was made.

She walked across the room slowly, her eyes never leaving his. She felt strange, disoriented, vulnerable when she stopped in front of him, for the first time allowing herself to just look at him in the stillness.

She was a tall woman, five feet nine in her bare feet, but he was far taller, six feet plus several inches. He still shouldn't have been intimidating. He wasn't bulky and bloated like a bodybuilder—his frame had the sleek, well-muscled grace of a long-distance runner. And he was hot, so very, very hot. And she'd been cold for so long.

He made no move to touch her. "Why do I frighten you, Molloy?" he asked, his voice low, enticing.

"What makes you think you do?"

His smile was slight, self-deprecatory. "Maybe I can read minds, as well."

It was a horrifying thought, one she dismissed almost immediately. If he knew even a fraction of the confused, downright lustful thoughts that had invaded her mind, he wouldn't be standing there, watching her, not touching her. If he could read her mind he'd have her down on the hardwood floor, her clothes scattered around them.

"You don't frighten me," she said.

"Don't lie." It was softly spoken, edged in steel.

"I'll do anything I please."

Again that faint, taunting smile. "Go right ahead," he murmured. "I dare you." And there was a glimmer of devilry in his dark eyes.

She was a tough woman. Not the sort to back down from a challenge. And Lord, the man was challenge personified. He was wrong—it wasn't him she was afraid of. It was herself, her reaction to him. Her undeniable vulnerability, when she'd spent so much time fighting any sign of weakness.

She tried to read his thoughts, but all she came up with was a frustrating blank. There was no safety net. The next move was up to her. Entirely.

She lifted her hands and touched him. She rested her fingertips against his shoulders for a moment, feeling him through the soft white cotton of his shirt.

The heat was a palpable thing, running through her fingertips, down her veins, burning like a glass of neat whiskey on a frosty afternoon. She broke the contact, stepping back, and she felt his cry of denial. But he didn't move, didn't say a word. He just waited. For her.

She wondered how long his patience would last. Not much longer than hers. She took a step back, toward him, and she knew that this time she wouldn't run.

"I don't want . . ." she began, then stopped.

"Don't want what? This?"

She shook her head. "I don't want to need you."

"Can you stop?"

"No." She reached up and put her hand against his mouth, and his lips were warm, burning. She wanted that mouth on her body.

He kissed her hand, gently. He reached out and took her other hand, bringing it slowly toward him, giving her plenty of chance to pull back. He placed it on his chest, over his heart, against his skin.

She could feel the beat of his pulse, heavy, sensual, slightly fast against her hand. Outside, the rain had begun once more, but inside they were safe and warm and dry.

She crossed the final step, coming up against his larger, hotter body, trapping their clasped hands between them. She moved her hand away from his lips and slid her fingers through his long dark hair, looking for answers in his dark, fathomless eyes.

But the answers weren't there to see, and she could either run or trust. And she'd decided she wasn't going to run.

He leaned down and kissed her then, very gently, a wordless reassurance that it was going to be all right. And she realized that, conscious decision or not, she trusted him. With her life. With her body. With her soul.

With her love.

She opened her mouth beneath his, deliberately inviting him. And then there was no gentle wooing. The heat that had been slumbering in his body flared up, and his mouth slanted across hers, drinking deep.

She could hear his thoughts then, a jumble of them, rioting through both their minds—dark, erotic, untamed, so fierce and so explicit in their demands that Suzanna felt her own response ignite. He slid his hands under her T-shirt, cupping her bare breasts, and she arched against him, needing his touch, needing his heat, needing his mouth.

He pulled the T-shirt over her head and sent it sailing across the room, and she was standing within his arms, wearing nothing but her jeans. She was no longer cold, she was burning up, and she wanted more, and more, and more.

He bent down and scooped her up effortlessly, holding her tight against him. You don't have to be tough all the time, his mind said, and she melted back against him, giving up the struggle for independence. He was right—she didn't have to fight anymore.

He took her over to the wide couch, lowering her down, following her, and she pushed the white shirt from his shoulders, her hands lingering, touching, learning him.

There were no words, no whispered assurances, no tiny jokes to set her at ease. In utter, absorbed silence he unfastened her jeans and pulled them down her legs, tossing them away. In silence he touched her, his long fingers sliding between her legs, coaxing them apart, and he leaned forward and put his mouth on her breast.

The sensation was fierce, burning, exquisite, and she heard her breathless cry of longing as she arched back against the soft cushions of the huge sofa. Her entire life centered between her legs and in her breast, and he was drawing the life from her, setting her on fire.

He moved his mouth to her other breast, suckling deeply, and she felt hot tears of longing and confusion fill her eyes, as she reached down for him, not sure of what she wanted, only certain that she did.

Her breast felt damp and cool when he moved his mouth away, trailing hot, biting kisses down her torso.

And then he put his mouth between her legs, unexpectedly soon, and she put her hands on his shoulders, unsure. He simply covered her hands with his, the heat of them soothing her doubts, and she let herself slip, slide into a dark and wonderful place, full of brazen images and unspoken desires, lost, whirling in a kind of mad splendor that sharpened into a blinding clarity as she climaxed against his mouth.

She was only vaguely aware of him moving up and over her, shucking his jeans, kneeling between her trembling legs. She waited, watching as he protected her, wanting to reach out and touch him, to do it for him, still too shaky and shy to move. And then he was pressing against her, sliding deep, filling her with one sure thrust, and he was so burning hot that she was burning with him, pushing her body against his, her long legs right around his hips, wanting more, wanting all of him, everything he was willing to give, resenting anything that came between them, even the thin barrier of latex.

His hands cupped her hips, pulling her more tightly against him. His mouth crushed hers, and she heard him, the words, sifting through his mind, love and lust and longing, striving for an end that was only a beginning. She clutched at him, shivering, building, shattering once more as she felt him explode in her arms, a white hot flame of passion that seemed to last an eternity.

When she opened her eyes, she found him collapsed on top of her, his long hair in her face, his heart still pounding furiously against her. He was heavy, and she didn't mind for even a moment.

She felt better than she had in her entire life. Her body was hot, nerveless, completely sated, her mind at ease. And her heart—her heart was full of an indescribable feeling that had a very simple definition.

And that was *love*.

She heard the word shift through his mind, unconsciously before it was pushed away in sudden fear. If she asked him for those words, he might give them to her, but it was no good asking. Those words had to be freely given, out of his need, not hers.

He lifted his head and looked at her, and she could feel his doubt. But she couldn't sense where that doubt had come from.

"Are you all right?" he asked, his voice barely more than a whisper.

He was worried he might have hurt her, that much was clear. She couldn't resist. There was no way she could stop the wide, smug grin that curved her mouth, any more than she could stop the warmth that filled her inside. "I'll survive," she said.

He stared at her for a long moment. And then he smiled too, a slow, sensuous grin that temporarily banished the shadows that lingered around them. He put his mouth against hers, offering a slow, lingering kiss. He was still deep inside her, and he was growing hard again, and she was growing damp and hot, and her hands slid around him as she kissed him back, losing herself in the sheer heaven of his mouth.

When he finally pulled away from her, she let him go reluctantly. "No," she said.

He paused, staring down at her. "No?" he echoed.

"No, you can't use a condom twice. At least, I don't think so," she added truthfully.

"I forgot you could read my mind."

"Not all the time."

"What else have I been thinking?"

She found, to her amazement, that she could blush. Lying beneath him in the shadowy living room, his aroused body still tight within hers, she could blush.

"I guess that's answer enough." He pulled away, slowly, reluctantly. "I'll be back." There was an old quilt over the arm of the sofa, and he tossed it around her naked body. "Don't go anywhere."

She snuggled down in the cushions, closing her eyes with a sigh. Odd, that temporary resentment of the protection he'd used. She was smart enough, mature enough to understand the necessity of it. But for the first time in her life she'd felt like a lovesick fool, wanting everything from her lover, willing to risk an unplanned pregnancy and worse in her need to be close to him.

He came back to her. She heard an odd sound, and looked up to see him drop a pile of red foil packets on the floor beside the couch before he knelt down beside her. "Second thoughts?" he asked. "Regrets?"

"Should I have?" she answered, trying to read his thoughts. But they were shuttered, impossible to detect.

He simply shook his head. "No," he said. "This has been a long time coming." He brushed her hair away from her face, then frowned. "You were crying."

"I suppose so."

"Did I hurt you? I'm not certain of my strength. You should have said something—"

She stopped his mouth, sitting up and letting the cover drop to her waist, putting her lips against his. She let her mouth rest gently against his, touching, tasting, her tongue sliding against his firm lips, letting his mouth open against hers so she could kiss him fully. When she pulled back, she managed a shaky smile. "I always cry when I'm happy," she said.

"And you were happy?"

"Very."

"How are you right now?"

"I could be happier."

His smile was slow, sensual, as he picked up her hand in his, his thumb stroking the back of it. "I have a few ideas," he murmured, and he put her hand on him, the silky strength of him, already hard for her.

Her fingers wrapped around him, gently, learning him, her fingertips soft and questing. "I have a few of my own, Dr. Crompton," she replied.

"I'm sure you do, Molloy," he said as his breath caught in reaction. "I imagine you can be extremely inventive."

"Try me."

"I have every intention of doing just that." And pulling the cover away from her, he pulled her body up against his, heat against heat, and his mouth covered hers.

THE RAIN STOPPED. The sky was still cloudy, and Suzanna rolled onto her back, looking out the roof window into the gathering dawn. She was still mostly asleep, her body floating in some wonderful daze of exhausted pleasure. She wondered where Daniel was. And then she knew.

She reached over and touched him. He was closer than she'd realized, but she didn't waken him. Or, at least, she could only assume she didn't. He made a snoring sort of grunt, and she felt the futon shift beneath them, and then she was wrapped in his arms once more, her cheek pressed up against his chest. A chest she couldn't see.

More's the pity, she thought idly, reaching her hand up to gently stroke his arm. He had a truly beautiful chest. She'd always thought she liked lots of hair on a man. He had very little, just bone and muscle and golden skin.

He'd carried her upstairs at one point during the night, and she couldn't be quite sure when. She'd been clinging to him, legs wrapped around his waist, and he'd been buried deep inside her as he mounted the stairs. They'd collapsed at the top, finishing there on the bare wood, and just managed to crawl to the bed. At some point they'd even ended up in the hot tub together, before collapsing into a deep, exhausted sleep.

She pressed her face against him, inhaling the scent of his skin, the lingering smell of the soap they'd used with erotic abandon. Outside, the world was a dark, threatening place. Inside, in this magical little house, everything was just wonderful.

She could smell a faint trace of gasoline. An odd scent, one she hadn't noticed before, and she wondered if it had anything to do with Daniel's peculiar powers. Was he somehow able to project something inflammable?

Her body had tensed, and he was awake beside her, his arms tightening around her. "What's wrong?" His voice was sleepy, just becoming alert.

"I thought I smelled gas. I wasn't sure. . . ."

"I smell it, too," he said, and she found herself released. "Someone's here."

He was already off the bed, and she had the eerie sensation of watching clothes float through the air as he grabbed them, then watched them disappear as he pulled them over his body. "Stay put," he ordered. "I'm going to check on things."

"The hell I will," she said, sitting up.

An invisible hand shoved her back against the pillows. "Don't be an idiot, Molloy. If someone's out there, they won't see me. They sure as hell will see you. Use your brain for once."

"You mean, as opposed to last night," she countered, stung.

She couldn't see him, but she could hear his thoughts. Feel his cool, angry withdrawal. "That's your decision," he said finally. "You can occupy your time figuring it out. But if you try to follow me, I swear I'll punch you."

"I always wanted an abusive lover."

"Suzanna..."

"Go away, Daniel. I'll be a good little girl and stay put."

She could feel his reluctant smile. "I thought no one was supposed to call you *girl.*"

She found she could smile, as well, despite her bad mood. "So I'm feeling a little girlish today. Go out and save the world, Cinderman. The little woman will be waiting with a hot meal."

She felt the air rush beside her, and then he kissed her, hard. She closed her eyes—it was too disorienting, being kissed by an invisible man. His kisses were shattering enough. She reached up to clutch his shoulders, but he slipped away from her.

"I knew I could count on you."

She leaned back on the mattress, unable to watch him leave. The bottom sheet was pulled halfway off, the duvet was on the floor, and she reached and pulled it over her. It was already cooler without him in the room. The temperature had dropped, and her inner warmth had turned to ice.

He was enjoying himself, damn it. She felt the excitement blazing through him as he went in search of the intruder. He was looking forward to this, a superhero confronting evil. She wanted to slap him. She wanted to clutch him and tell him to be careful, for God's sake. She wanted to lie in bed with the covers over her head and pray for him to return safely.

She heard the door open, the footsteps in the big room below, and she rose from the bed, leaning over the balcony with the duvet clutched around her, ready to offer him a provocative invitation. The words died in her throat as she recognized the man beneath her, wandering through Daniel's precious house, his elegant, cruel hands rifling through the papers and books that littered the place.

He didn't look up, didn't realize she stood there, watching him in bemused horror. "Where the hell are you, Crompton?" he muttered under his breath, slamming open the door to the lab.

No answer, of course, and no sign of him. Suzanna wondered if he was in the house, or if he was outside, looking for their intruder.

And would he realize the man inside was a far cry from the civilized businessman he appeared to be?

Looking down at Henry Osborn's pale, pink head, she could only hope so.

Chapter Fourteen

Suzanna backed away from the balcony as silently as she could. Her clothes lay scattered on the living room floor beneath her, but she was able to rifle through her duffel bag and come up with another pair of jeans and a T-shirt. She'd just pulled it over her head when she felt the eyes on her, and she knew they weren't Daniel's unseen eyes.

She turned, slowly, taking a deep breath to control her sudden panic. He was standing there, blocking the narrow stairway, and he looked impeccable, unruffled, despite the smell of gasoline that clung to him.

"We've been looking for you, Ms. Molloy," he said in a charming, genial voice. "You know, I didn't believe Daniel when he told me you two had something going, but I guess I was wrong. You certainly have a well-screwed look."

She barely blinked at his deliberate crudeness. "What are you doing here, Mr. Osborn?"

"You were awake two nights ago, weren't you?" He took a step closer, a small, sadistic smile on his face. "I thought you might be, even though you managed to hide it. Maybe you have a taste for pain."

"Not particularly." She sounded very cool, something she could congratulate herself on. Of course, she felt more than cool. She felt chilled to the bone.

"Don't make this difficult, Ms. Molloy. Where is he?"

"Where is who?"

He closed his eyes, sighing in genteel exasperation. "I don't mind doing my own dirty work, you know," he confided. "It's been years since I've been in the trenches, but an old soldier never loses his touch. If for no other reason, this latest debacle has been instructive. But I don't care to prolong it any further. I have people who want answers, and I intend to provide them. Where is Dr. Crompton?"

"Didn't you see him when you came in?"

"No."

"We heard you," she said in a dulcet voice. "He went in search of you. I wouldn't be surprised if you walked right past him and didn't see him."

"Not likely," he said with a snort. "I'm going to want you to come downstairs, Ms. Molloy. Very slowly and carefully—no sudden moves or shouts for help."

"Why should I?"

"Because I have a gun. I know how to use it. I'm actually quite good with it," he said in a calm, measured voice. "I think I would start by shooting you in the throat. That way you wouldn't be able to call for assistance."

She hadn't even noticed the gun in his hand. It was small, black and undoubtedly capable of doing all he said and more. She put an involuntary hand up to her throat, and his smile widened.

"Come along, Ms. Molloy. Let's go downstairs and wait for Dr. Crompton to return."

"What if he's left?" she asked, moving slowly, carefully ahead of him, down the narrow flight of stairs. "What if he's gone for help?"

"Where could he go? There's no one around for miles. If it weren't for my contacts, we would never have found this place."

"We?" She took a brief, surreptitious glance around the living room. It was cold down there, icy, and she knew that Daniel must still be outside. The smell of the gasoline was even stronger downstairs, and there was no way she could dismiss her sense of impending doom.

"Surely you must realize by now that Beebe has limitless resources. The finest minds, the greatest talents of this country, have lent themselves to Beebe, and I can say quite truthfully that there's no stopping us."

"No stopping you from what?"

Osborn smiled like a rat. "Have a seat while we wait for the good doctor."

He gestured with the gun, and Suzanna didn't make the mistake of thinking she had any choice in the matter. She took the seat he pointed at, putting her hands in her lap and trying to still her panic. "No stopping you from what?" she asked again.

"Our noble cause. Our patriotic duty. We're not fools, Ms. Molloy, even if Washington seems to be overrun these days with bleeding-heart liberals. Those who ignore their history are doomed to repeat it. If we're fools enough to seek isolation, to let those third-world countries fend for themselves, then we're asking for the collapse of the United States as a world power."

"I didn't know we were letting them fend for themselves," she began, watching warily as Osborn drew a thin nylon cord out of his perfectly tailored pocket.

"The hell with economic help or economic sanctions. Blackmail won't get us what we want," he said, tucking the gun in his pocket and advancing on her, the nylon cord extended. "Arms. Weapons. That's the only power these people will understand."

"How does Dr. Crompton fit into that?" She tensed herself. She could fight back. He wasn't any taller than she was, and he was a great deal older. She had a chance against him, as long as he put that gun away.

"He's brilliant. Quite our most valuable asset. We assumed he was working on cold fusion, and if he'd managed to perfect it we would have been in the catbird seat."

"Then why were you trying to kill him?"

Osborn looked disgruntled. "We were fed the wrong information. That fool Jackson said he'd perfected it, that he was only a liability. If Crompton suffered from a fatal lab accident, there'd be no one to interfere with our plans for cold fusion."

"Wouldn't that be killing the goose that laid the golden egg?" she asked, and in the far recesses of her mind she heard Crompton's disgruntled reaction to being called a goose.

"We wouldn't have needed him any longer. He's not the only brilliant scientist in the world. With his research, we could have hired other, more practical men, and gone on to develop a power base such as the world has never seen."

"But things went wrong."

Osborn grimaced. "Thank God. Once Jackson had time to put all the research together, we knew we were in trouble. Whatever Crompton was working on, it had nothing to do with cold fusion. It didn't resemble anything anyone could recognize."

"So why don't you kill him?"

"I'm not a fool, Ms. Molloy. I didn't get where I am today by ignoring potential. He's America's secret weapon. Whatever that amazing brain has come up with will be worth billions. Trillions. The entire national debt. I'm taking him back with me, if I can."

"And if you can't?"

He smiled. "Then sooner or later someone will be able to take his research and make sense of it."

"What are you going to do with me?"

"Why, nothing at all, my dear. Just tie you up so you won't interfere. I promise I won't tie you so tightly that you won't be able to loosen your bonds within a couple of hours."

She shook her head. "What makes you the executioner, Mr. Osborn? I would have thought that duty would be left for underlings. Or do you have a taste for killing?"

"My dear girl," he said in his unctuous voice, "I don't usually waste my time with enforcement duties. But this has partly been my responsibility, letting things get out of hand like this, and I want to make sure things are handled right from now on. Besides, I have a certain talent." He was standing close enough that she could smell his cologne, mixed with the scent of gasoline. It was very elegant, expensive cologne. Her father had used it, as well. "Put your hands at your sides, my dear, and I promise I won't tie them too tightly."

She looked up at him. Where was Crompton? "That answers one question," she said, keeping her hands folded in her lap, her muscles coiled to spring.

"What's that?"

"You're not planning on putting that rope around my wrists. You're planning on strangling me with it."

She'd managed to shock him out of his slimy equanimity. "My dear girl," he protested, moving closer, the nylon rope stretched tight between his two soft white hands.

"I can read your mind," she said savagely. "And don't call me *girl!*"

He lunged for her then, but she was too fast for him, ducking and rolling out of the chair, onto the hard wood floor. "Daniel!" she screamed as Osborn fell on top of her, the rope snaking around her throat.

She grabbed at it with her hands, but the man was murderously strong, brutally efficient. His knee pressed into her back as he wrapped the rope twice around her neck.

Time stood still. Years ago she'd read an article about a woman who'd almost been strangled to death by a maniac. She'd been saved, but the loss of oxygen to her brain had left her in a wheelchair, her nerves and muscles useless. Suzanna clawed at the rope, trying to scream again, but it was too tight. No sound came out, and she knew she was going to die. Better that than to be left a living corpse. But she hadn't been able to tell Daniel she loved him, she loved him . . .

The weight disappeared from her back with shocking speed, the tension slackened from the rope around her throat, and she yanked it away, coughing and choking, barely aware of her surroundings. And then she heard Osborn babbling.

She sat up, dazed. The man who'd tried to strangle her lay spread-eagled on the floor, a look of glazed horror on his face. "What's going on here?" he gasped.

"I'm going to kill you, Osborn." Daniel's voice came from thin air, cool, unyielding, deadly.

Osborn stared around him, trying to see the source of that voice. "Where are you, Crompton?" he demanded, getting back some of his bluster. "You know I wasn't really going to hurt the girl. I was just trying to scare her."

"Don't call her *girl*," Daniel said in a tight, lethal voice. "Thirty seconds more and she would have passed out. Another minute and she would have suffered permanent brain damage. But you weren't going to hurt her, were you, Hank?" His voice was savage as he called the dignified old man by his totally inappropriate nickname. "Any more than you were going to hurt her when you mauled her in the hospital. Where did you get your training, Osborn? You're too young to be a Nazi, even if you have the personality for it."

Osborn sat up, his equilibrium momentarily back in place. "It's some kind of remote speaker, isn't it?" he said with renewed self-confidence. "And just so you don't underestimate me, I should tell you I got my training with the best. The CIA taught me everything I know. Now where are you, Crompton, and how did you manage to throw me? Was it some sort of electric shock?" He brushed a speck of dust off his rumpled jacket.

An invisible hand punched him in his shoulder, knocking him backward. "It's a shock, all right," Daniel said. "Suzanna, I want you to get out of here."

She'd managed to pull herself together, just barely. Her throat was on fire, and the smell of gasoline was growing even stronger. "I won't let you kill him, Daniel," she said.

"You can't stop me."

"Daniel, if you kill him, you'll become just like him."

"Do you think I give a damn? I don't spend my life worrying about petty notions of morality. He hurt you, he was going to kill you—"

"Daniel . . ."

"Get out of here."

Osborn lay back on the rug. "Don't leave me," he croaked. "I don't know what's going on here, but don't leave me alone."

"The problem is, Osborn, that you're not alone," Daniel said in a silken voice, close enough to him that Osborn must have felt his breath on his face.

Osborn jumped a mile, scuttling backward till he came up against the wall. "Is this what you've been working on? Some kind of invisible ray?"

"It's the side effect of that little lab explosion you and Jackson manufactured for me," he said. "Just one of the benefits of hazardous work. By the way, did you kill Jackson, or was it Armstead's little army?"

Osborn's color was ghastly. He stared straight ahead, like a blind man. "It's hot here," he choked, loosening his tie.

"It was you, wasn't it? You've got a taste for such things. I'm sure Armstead didn't tell you to come and kill Suzanna. You just decided to show a little initiative."

"I don't take orders from Armstead."

"Oh, but you do. You're an errand boy, Osborn. A figurehead for Big Brother, doing what they tell you, taking your punishment like a man. Are you ready to die?"

"Daniel!" Suzanna shrieked in protest.

Osborn lurched to his feet, throwing himself toward the sound of Daniel's voice, arms outstretched to topple him. He connected with nothing and went down hard.

He lay there, panting, and when he tried to rise, something in the middle of his back shoved him downward again. Suzanna could only suppose it was Daniel's foot.

"I'm not the only one who's going to die," he wheezed, his face twisted and malevolent. "You're going with me, and your girlfriend, as well."

"Who have you got waiting for us, Osborn?" Daniel's voice was silky with menace. "One of Armstead's mercenaries?"

"I don't need anyone. This place is set to blow, and I'm the only one who can stop it. Get off me, and this whole conversation will be academic." Osborn tried to get up, but the invisible foot stayed planted in the center of his back.

"How long?"

Osborn's pale face had a grimace of triumph. "Let me up," he said again. "Or the girlfriend goes up with us."

"Bastard," Daniel muttered, but Suzanna could sense him move away from the prone man. It shouldn't have come as a surprise when unseen hands wrapped around her arms and hauled her to her feet. "Get out of here, Suzanna. Get down the hill as fast as you can, and keep your eyes open for any of his little buddies."

"Not without you," she said in a raw, rasping voice.

"I'll be right behind you."

"How will I know that?" she said stubbornly. Henry Osborn had managed to climb to his feet, and he stood there, swaying, his perfect white hair mussed, his elegantly groomed face a mask of violent rage.

"You'll have to trust me." Daniel's hands were strong, unyielding, as they pushed her toward the door.

She was still fighting him, even knowing that she was a dangerous distraction. "Are you going to kill him?" she demanded in a hoarse whisper.

She heard his long-suffering sigh, and she could just imagine the expression on his face. She put out her hand and touched him, connecting with his cheek, brushing against his mouth in a last caress.

"He deserves it," he muttered. "If I weren't such a sentimental fool, I'd throw him over the balcony."

For me, she wanted to ask, but was afraid to.

For you, he thought, and she heard it, even though he wouldn't say the words aloud. And she smiled up at him. "I'll wait for you at the bottom of the path." Then she was gone.

"She's not going to get very far, Crompton," Osborn said in a casual voice. He'd straightened his silk tie, and his pale pink hands weren't even shaking.

Daniel turned from his spot by the door. He knew what Osborn had in mind. As long as he could engage him in conversation, he could pinpoint his location. Daniel had no intention of giving him that edge.

"Haven't you realized by now just how far-reaching Beebe is? You scientists, with your dreams and your heads in the clouds... you don't have any idea what real power is all about. Beebe is about power. There's no place she'll be safe. Even if you lied to her, and I don't make it down this hillside, Armstead and his men will be waiting. If she doesn't go back to Santa Cristina, they'll still find her. It may take a while, but those men are dedicated. Sooner or later they'll run her to ground, and they'll wipe her existence off the face of the earth."

Daniel moved slowly, silently toward the sliding doors leading onto the narrow balcony. He'd have to pass Osborn to get out there, and while he knew he could manage to accomplish that without making any noise, he was afraid his body heat would give him away.

But he had to get out of there. Osborn assumed he hadn't noticed the innocuous little box tucked into a corner of the deck, or the almost transparent wires leading away from it. He'd underestimated his opponent, a fatal mistake. Daniel wasn't a man who missed anything, and he'd noticed that box instantly. He had to get rid of it, or the whole house that he'd built with his bare hands would be a pile of cinders. And he'd probably be in the ashes, as well.

Osborn took a step, blocking the center of the door. "I'm afraid not, Crompton. You've become too great a liability, despite your undeniable gifts. I'm afraid your usefulness is at an end. It's a pity, too. For a man with your intellect, you could have had anything you wanted. You always struck me as such a ruthless, practical man. You've changed."

Daniel was standing directly in front of him. "Yes," he said finally.

Osborn jumped, but recovered himself with impressive speed. "You've become practically human," he observed. "What in God's name happened to you? Don't tell me you've been fool enough to fall in love with that girl?"

"Don't call her a girl," Daniel said absently.

"Is that it? Has true love made an idiot out of you?"

"Not exactly," Daniel drawled. "It was more likely a case of green slime."

He heard the change. The quiet, merciless little hum of the box on the porch suddenly went into a high-pitched squeal, so painful that Daniel held his ears for a moment. Osborn didn't move, obviously deaf to the sound.

He didn't have any time to waste. "Out of my way," he snarled, shoving at him. He'd forgotten Osborn's training. Those deceptively soft hands shot out and caught him, and Osborn managed to pull him off balance, before Daniel loosened himself and tossed the man away.

Unfortunately he tossed him toward the glass doors. Osborn went crashing through, landing in a heap on top of the incendiary device. For a moment Daniel didn't move, hoping to God Osborn was knocked unconscious, hoping that for once Suzanna had listened to him and made her way down the hill, hoping that there was some way out of this mess that had blown up out of nowhere.

Osborn rose, the box in his hand. "I always wanted to die for my country," he said, a fanatic light gleaming in his eye. "Crompton," he murmured, "you're toast."

Instinct took over. Daniel hadn't realized he could move so fast. He could hear the metal contacts click together just as he leapt over the balcony. The force of the blast sent him head over heels, and then he was falling, falling, over and over, through the tall pines, down the steep cliff to the rocky ledge below. The flames were behind him, shooting into the sky, black and inky, and he knew Osborn was dead. As he would be, once he hit the ground.

He could hear her scream of disbelieving horror. And then everything went black, as the granite ledge rushed up to meet him, and his last thought was a faint regret that he'd never told Suzanna he was in love with her. And now it was too late.

SUZANNA SANK TO HER KNEES in the mud. "No," she moaned. "No, no, no." But there was no answer to her strangled cries. Just the crackle of the blazing house as the fire consumed it, and the cry of the wind in the trees overhead.

"Daniel," she whispered, but there was no answer. She scrambled to her feet, clawing her way back up to where the house had stood. The heat was suffocating, the smoke choking, the house caving in on itself. "Daniel," she screamed in her raw voice, but there was no answer. In that tiny clearing that had once held a magic cottage and now held only a blazing inferno, there was no one left alive to hear her.

Chapter Fifteen

Suzanna had no idea how long she knelt in the clearing, blasted by the heat of the burning building, or what made her struggle to her feet. She moved back down the narrow trail like a robot, her mind a deliberate blank. She had only one thought. Daniel was dead, and she had to run—away from the men who killed him, and away from the knowledge of his death. She needed to run as far and as fast as she could, find some place to crawl into. And then maybe she could mourn.

The Jaguar sat parked at the bottom of the hill, directly over the spot where Jackson's sedan had been incinerated. Daniel would have liked to have made ashes of that car, as well, with Osborn inside. She wondered whether he'd started the fire. If he had, it would have been an accident. Despite the ruthlessness in his voice, he wouldn't have murdered Osborn in cold blood. And he wouldn't have destroyed his beautiful house.

Osborn must have rigged something, determined to destroy them all. And she had escaped.

It was no comfort, none at all. She stared at the hunter-green luxury car and wondered what kind of luck she'd have hot-wiring the thing. She opened the passenger door, expecting the blare of antitheft devices. Instead she got a discreet little buzz, so quiet and well-bred that it took her a dazed moment to realize that Osborn had left the keys in the ignition.

She slid into the driver's seat and slammed the door behind her. It was blisteringly hot in the car, oddly so, considering the early morning hour. She jerked the seat forward and turned the key, half expecting the car to explode. It started with a throaty purr, and she tore back down the narrow, rutted dirt road with a complete disregard for the elegant car she drove.

She punched on the air-conditioning. Her hands were trembling, her mind a careful blank. All she wanted to do was drive, and keep on driving, as far away from her conscious thoughts as she could go.

For a moment she closed her eyes, trying to hear Daniel's thoughts, to find out for sure if he was really dead. Nothing answered her, not even the breath of an emotion. Daniel Crompton was gone, wiped out, incinerated from the face of this earth. Cinderman was cinders.

She heard the faint moan of anguish, and she shoved a fist in her mouth to quiet it. She couldn't let go now. She had to get away, as fast as she possibly could. She just had to wait until she found a place to hide.

It was still unbearably hot. The heat was coming from the empty back seat, and she wondered whether the heating system in the car was malfunctioning, sending warmth out the back ducts. She couldn't afford to spend the time checking. She cranked the air-conditioning higher, shoved her bare foot down on the accelerator and kept going, pulling out onto the narrow paved road with a skid of tires.

The blessed numbness lasted less than an hour. It lasted until she happened to glance at the digital clock on the leather-and-wood dashboard, in time to see that it was now only eight o'clock. The conflagration at the cabin had happened in a deathly short period of time. It was the hour for Daniel to regain his visibility. But Daniel was gone—there was no more body to appear.

The first sob took her by surprise, shaking her body. The second one was even worse, tearing her apart, and out of sheer self-preservation she slowed her manic speed, as the tears streamed down her face and her body was racked with sobs. "I can't stand it," she wept, pounding the steering wheel. "He can't be dead." She glanced in the rearview mirror, to make sure no one was pulling up behind her as she crept along the road, her body shaking with misery.

In the rearview mirror appeared the disheveled face of Daniel Crompton. "I'm not," he said blandly.

Suzanna promptly ran into a tree.

What little self-control she'd still owned disappeared as the car stalled out, and she buried her face in her hands. She heard the rear door open, heard her own driver's door open, but when he put his hands on her she lost it completely, screaming at him, beating at him, fury and pain and relief exploding from her in a wild rage.

He was so strong. He simply pulled her into his arms, out of the car, held her flailing fists with one hand, tucking her against him as he sank down on the grass. And then she began to weep, great ugly sobs that tore her apart.

He said nothing. His body was strong and so hot that it spread warmth through her suddenly chilled flesh. His hand was soothing her tangled hair.

She had no idea how long her crying fit lasted. The spasms that racked her body slowed, then stumbled to a halt, and she was simply lying in his arms, weak, wasted, the tears finally gone.

"I hate you," she said in a small, pained voice.

"Why?" It was an eminently logical question, what she'd expect from him. Even as his hands were stroking her, soothing her.

"Because you let me think you were dead. You somehow managed to sneak away and hide in the back of the car, and you never said a word...."

"I didn't sneak away," he said. "I jumped over the balcony when Osborn detonated the device he'd rigged."

She lifted her head. Her face was wet with tears, and he smoothed them away with his deft thumbs. "You couldn't have," she said. "It was a sheer drop, onto granite. You'd be dead."

He shrugged. "Interesting, isn't it? I blacked out, but I'm most assuredly not dead. I feel kind of stiff and sore, but apart from that I'm in one piece. I managed to crawl to Henry's car, but I'm afraid I passed out in the back seat. I wasn't in any shape to say anything."

She looked at him in awe. "Does that mean you're invulnerable, as well? You can't die?"

The idea didn't seem to please him. "I have no idea. Obviously I can survive a fall like that. We'll simply have to find someplace where I can experiment a bit more. Damn," he said abruptly.

"What?"

"The specimen I was working on. It's gone."

"So is the house," she said mournfully. She'd loved that house.

He shrugged. "Houses can be rebuilt. I don't know how I'll ever find more green slime. Unless Beebe has some squirreled away. I want an antidote, and I'm not going to come up with one if I can't figure out what it was in the first place."

She managed a watery smile. "You mean you don't want to be Cinderman after all?"

"Not particularly. What about you?" he asked, pushing her hair away from her tear-damp face. "You want to spend the rest of your life doing a mind-reading act?"

"No," she said, just looking at him, at the face she'd never expected to see again. "But I do like going without my glasses."

He managed a wry grin. "Maybe we'll let you keep your powers. You feel ready to continue on?"

For a moment she didn't move. "Where are we going?"

"Back to Santa Cristina. They're not going to let us be, Molloy. We can't keep running. I've got to go back and face them."

"What about me?"

"I'll take you someplace safe, if we can think of it."

She shook her head. "I'm staying with you." She ought to tell him. She'd almost lost him once—now was the time to tell him.

But she couldn't. He sat there looking at her, cool and composed, despite the streak of dirt on his face and the twigs and leaves in his long hair. He wasn't the kind of man she could easily say "I love you" to. He'd probably ask her to define it scientifically.

She smiled wryly. "Any objections?" she added.

"Would you listen to them?"

"Nope."

"Then I'll save my breath. Let's get moving. I want to be off the road by six o'clock."

She climbed off him reluctantly, wondering if she was imagining the way his hands clung to her for a moment before releasing her. Wondering if he'd thought of her when he vaulted over the balcony to what should have been a certain death below.

"Do you want to tell me what happened back there?" she asked. "Did you start the fire?"

He looked bleak for a moment. "No," he said. "To both questions. I'll drive."

She could have argued, but in truth, her knees were weak, her hands were trembling, and all she wanted to do was crawl into the soft leather seat of the Jaguar and look at him. "All right," she said.

He threw her a mocking glance. "Docile all of a sudden, are we? What happened to the tough creature who ate male chauvinist pigs for breakfast?"

She glanced down at the T-shirt she'd grabbed in the darkness: The Truth Shall Set You Free, But First It Will Piss You Off. Apt enough for today. "She's tired," Suzanna said wearily. "I'll be more than ready to go ten rounds when we get back to California."

"I'll be looking forward to it."

DANIEL DECIDED he didn't like Jaguars. Or, at least, he didn't like this particular one. Not that it didn't have plenty of power, a smooth ride and a decent radio. It even came equipped with a CD player, but since the late Henry Osborn's taste in music had tended toward marching bands and motivational tapes, he made do with the FM.

But it had a soft, leathery bucket seat, and Suzanna lay curled up, miles away in her own soft, leathery bucket seat. And he wanted her curled up next to him, with her head in his lap, her blond hair spread over his thighs.

It had been quite a night. So active that he should have used up his sexual energy for the next six months. He'd certainly used up his supply of condoms.

So it made no sense that the very sight of her, the sound of her soft breathing, the scent of her, would be driving him crazy with lust.

And that's all it was, he told himself self-righteously. That's all he believed in. Chemistry, animal attraction. For some reason he and the cantankerous Suzanna Molloy made a perfect match. It wouldn't last, of course. But it certainly was far stronger than anything he'd felt in his entire life.

He suspected it was the same for her. For a moment he wished he had her uncanny ability to read other people's thoughts. He would have liked to know what went on behind those warm, wary brown eyes when she looked at him. She hadn't come to bed with him like a woman who was used to that sort of thing. She'd been hesitant, shy, disarmingly so. Out of bed she was a tiger—in his arms she was surprisingly unsure.

He was used to sexual athletes. Wonderwomen, who knew what they wanted and how to achieve it with the minimum of fuss. Suzanna had been uncertain, and he'd had to woo her, each time breaking down her resistance.

He wondered whether he was going to have to woo her when they got back to Santa Cristina. Or whether he'd be able to stop her in the first lonely place he found and take her standing up, her legs wrapped around his hips, her nails digging into his back.

He adjusted his jeans, shifting in the seat, and glanced over at her. She was asleep, and he could see the pale mauve shadows beneath her eyes. She needed to be left alone, to recoup her strength and self-assurance. The past twenty-four hours had thrown her off balance, from lying on her back beneath him to watching the house explode into flames, thinking he was inside.

He had never stopped to consider what it might mean to her. He'd never thought that someone might care so much if he met a fiery end. His own elderly parents would most likely accept it as they accepted everything. With calm, measured practicality. His parents weren't much for emotion, only intellect, and now that they were in their late seventies they seemed absolute strangers to any kind of feeling. They'd mourn, of course, but probably more for the waste of potential than for their only son.

But Suzanna hadn't accepted his supposed loss with equanimity, or even a sentimental tear or two. She'd been shattered, and that rage of emotion, of raw feeling, frightened him as little else could. He didn't want to mean that much to anyone.

He glanced over at her. He could still see the salty traces of the tears that had run down her pale face. He didn't want her to love him. It complicated things, it made him uneasy, unsure, and at a time when he needed to concentrate all his energies, all his intellect, on stopping Beebe.

He turned his face away, staring out into the bright midday light as he drove south toward California and fate. He didn't believe in love, and he didn't have time for it. He'd have to make that abundantly clear to Suzanna Molloy. What they had together was a certain argumentative compatibility and a powerful sexual communication. It didn't have to be cloaked in hearts and flowers. It wasn't love.

She shifted next to him, and he started guiltily. "Did you know," she said, her voice cool and clear, "that I could hear some of Osborn's thoughts?"

"Interesting," he replied.

"Not as clearly as yours, though. Only a thought or two filtered through from him. Whereas with you I tend to hear far too much." It was a warning, gently spoken.

"Suzanna," he said, suddenly feeling like the lowest creature of all creation.

"You might turn the radio up," she said quietly. "That might drown some of it out."

He leaned forward and did so, and the annoying sound of rap music filled the elegant car. It was probably the first time in its short history the car had been subjected to such an indignity. He deliberately envisioned her, naked, lying beneath him, legs spread and waiting, and he glanced over to see her reaction.

No telltale blush. No reaction whatsoever. "That's better," she murmured, closing her eyes again.

"We need to talk."

"Not now," she said, turning her back on him. He could see the straight line of her spine beneath her T-shirt. It looked strong, it looked angry, it looked vulnerable.

He'd give her time. And deliberately he concentrated on the antiestablishment, kill-the-Man rhetoric on the radio. For once it was something he could identify with.

He drove steadily through the day. The only time Suzanna emerged from the cocoon she'd spun about herself was when he stopped at a fast-food restaurant. Even the sight of a hamburger and french fries couldn't bring back the light in her eyes, but at least she managed to eat an indecent amount. She said nothing about his choice of salad and milk shake, and he missed her razzing him. But he had the good sense to give her time and space. He simply looked at his salad and calculated how many grams of fat were in the dressing, shielding his thoughts from her.

It was just after five when he pulled the car to a stop. It was getting dark already, the autumn light fading quickly, and he killed the motor, waiting for Suzanna to emerge from her daylong retreat.

"Where are we?" she asked, looking around sleepily.

"About ten miles from Beebe, if you take back roads and go across country a bit."

"Lord," she moaned. "Don't tell me you're still trying to get me to walk?"

"No. There's an old place back in the woods here. I was thinking of buying it. We can hide out here for a while, at least until after eight."

She looked at him curiously. "Why don't you want to go there until eight? Aren't you wasting any possible advantage you might have?"

"No." He'd figured it all out while she slept. If he went in while he was invisible, he would simply be leaving Suzanna as the only available target. He already knew he wouldn't be able to get her to stay behind, short of binding and gagging her, and he didn't think she'd let him get away with that.

She smiled wryly. "Thanks."

"For what?"

"For your chivalry."

He slammed his hand against the steering wheel. "You know what it's like, having a voyeur peering at my every thought?"

"Hey, I don't like it, either," she snapped back, her tentative smile vanishing. "And it's not your every thought. It's just the occasional one."

"It's still too damned many."

"I agree."

Silence, heated, angry, filling the car. "Let's get out of here," he said finally. "I don't know whether anyone noticed us as we got nearer Santa Cristina. It's a distinctive car."

She accepted the peace offering, for what it was, unfastening the seat belt and sliding out of the front seat. "Lead on, MacDuff. Let's just hope we can find some food at this place."

"I wouldn't count on it. Besides, you ate an indecent amount at the burger place."

"Most people eat more than once every twenty-four hours," she said in a deceptively tranquil voice.

He bit back his instinctive retort. The driveway of the old house was overgrown, neglected for the last few years as the old lady owner of the house had grown older and less observant. With the approaching dusk and the hunter green of the car, it would most likely escape detection, unless someone was looking for it at that particular place, which wasn't at all likely. As of Thursday afternoon, the old house had been on the market for more than six months, and he was the only one who'd shown the slightest bit of interest.

She said nothing as he led her up the winding driveway to the front door. He wasn't sure what he expected from her. She looked up at the deserted house with a bleak expression on her face, and he would have given anything for the momentary ability to read her thoughts.

"Stay here," he said. "I'll go around and let you in."

"You have a key?"

He didn't bother lying to her. "I know the easiest way to break in."

If he expected an argument, he didn't get one. She waited there, patient, quiet, until he opened the front door and drew her into the dusty little hallway.

"The power's still on," he said. "There's a television, if you're so inclined, and some of the furniture is still here, the worthless stuff. According to the real estate agent the antiques were already sold to—"

"You're babbling," Suzanna said, moving past him. "It's very nice."

He shut his mouth. "Yes," he said briefly. She was obviously having a monumental case of sulks because he wouldn't tell her he was in love with her, and it wasn't fair, just because he didn't believe in such things . . .

"Would you stop it!" she snapped, her temper frayed.

"Stop what?"

"Stop obsessing about not being in love with me! Did I ask you to? Have I been throwing myself at you, declaring my undying devotion, insisting on promises and vows of eternal love? Have I?" she demanded furiously.

"No."

"Then why do you keep fussing about it? I don't expect you to love me. I'm certain you're entirely incapable of it. We're good in bed, right? What was that lovely phrase you thought of—a certain argumentative compatibility? Why don't we just strip off our clothes and do it and stop arguing about imaginary things like being in love."

She looked magnificent, standing there in the dusky shadows, her breasts rising and falling beneath the

T-shirt. She looked like the answer to his every dream and more.

"I need a copy of that T-shirt," he said abruptly.

He'd manage to startle her. "What T-shirt?"

"The one you wore when I saw you for the first time. At the press conference, last summer. Denial Is Not Just a River in Egypt."

She just stared at him for a moment. "You remember that?"

"I remember everything about you."

"What are you trying to tell me?"

"Nothing I'm ready to say right now." He moved away from her, coward that he was, and she let him go. "We'll wait here until after eight o'clock. I'm not sure what we'll do till then...."

But she was gone. He heard her footsteps on the bare wood floors, and he wondered if she was running away from him. He'd have to go after her—it wasn't safe. And if he went after her, he might say what he didn't mean, didn't believe in, wasn't ready for...

"Hell and damnation," he muttered. His brain must have melted under the assault of green slime.

He went into the hallway, following her. She'd gone up the sharply angled staircase—he could hear her in the distance, his oddly acute hearing tuned in to her breathing. He heard the creak of a bed, the rustle of clothing, and he started after her.

The cramp hit him halfway up the second flight, sharp and hard, and he cursed, something brief and obscene, sagging against the wall, waiting for the pain to pass, waiting for his body to fade into nothingness. He didn't hear her come, but he looked up and she was standing there at the top of the stairs, looking down at him as he held his stomach.

"It must be almost six," she said.

He shut his eyes for a moment. "I'll go for a walk," he said. "As soon as this stops . . ."

She came up beside him and put her arm through his, tugging him gently upward. "Stop fighting, Daniel."

"What do you mean?"

"You need to rest. Stop fighting the pain, stop fighting me. Come and lie down. I'll wake you up when it's eight. It'll be easy enough to tell," she added with a wry smile.

He looked at her. He was already beginning to fade, and he could see from the determined expression on her face that she wasn't going to let that bother her. She tugged, and he went. She was right—he needed to stop fighting.

"That's right," she murmured soothingly. "Just give it up for a couple of hours." She pulled him into the bedroom at the top of the stairs, and by the time he was through the door he was invisible. "On the bed," she ordered.

It was most likely a horribly uncomfortable old bed. Even the old lady's heirs hadn't wanted it. It was a sagging double bed, with a concave mattress covered by faded ticking, and a plain barred iron headboard that looked as if it belonged in a reformatory. It looked like heaven.

"Just an hour," he agreed, sinking down on it and closing his eyes in relief. "Wake me at seven, and we'll talk."

"I don't want to talk to you, Daniel," she said. "I don't think I'm going to like anything you have to say. Go to sleep," she said firmly.

He opened his eyes for a moment. She was standing at the foot of the bed, her eyes shadowed. "What are you going to do?"

"Wake you when it's eight o'clock," she said gently. And she turned and left the room.

He had never felt so alone in his life. The narrow double bed was huge. He wanted to call after her, to tell her—

The words stopped. She didn't want to hear them. In his mind, in his voice.

And for once, she was right. He needed to sleep. He'd just about exhausted every last ounce of his reserves.

He'd wake himself up at seven. And then he'd make her listen.

Chapter Sixteen

Suzanna leaned forward and clicked off the black-and-white television set. Mistake number one was turning it on in the first place. She'd done so just in time to hear about the unfortunate demise of Henry Osborn, Daniel Crompton and his unnamed female companion in a fire of suspicious origin, up in an uninhabited tract of woodland in eastern Oregon.

Uncle Vinnie would be frantic. Not to mention Daniel's elderly parents. The phones were disconnected, and for a brief moment she considered taking the car and driving to the nearest pay phone, just long enough to set Uncle Vinnie's mind at ease.

And then she remembered what car they had. She hadn't looked, but if Henry Osborn's car didn't come equipped with a cellular phone, she'd turn invisible herself.

It was after seven when she came back from the car. It had taken her ages to figure out how to work the damned thing, and then Uncle Vinnie had asked all sorts of questions that she hadn't been prepared to answer. She'd finally ended up hanging up on him, after she'd gotten his promise to track down Daniel's parents and inform them that their son was very much alive. It was the least she could do. She remembered how it felt, twelve hours ago, when she'd knelt in the dirt and mourned his death. She couldn't let that happen to another human being, not without just cause.

The house was still and silent when she came back in, closing the door behind her. She was cold—she only had her T-shirt and jeans and bare feet, and the night air was brisk. She looked around for some kind of heat, then realized the most potent form of it was upstairs, asleep. All she had to do was go up to that bedroom and sit in the chair, and Daniel's inner blaze would warm her chilled bones.

She left the lights off as she went upstairs. The shadows had their customary, unnerving effect, but she decided to play it safe. Despite the fact that the house was deep within the woods, someone might come looking. Now that Uncle Vinnie knew she was somewhere near by, he might be foolish enough to mount a rescue attempt. She didn't want to involve him any more than she had to.

There was a full moon rising beyond the dusty, multi-paned window, and it shone on the empty bed. Except that it wasn't empty at all. She stood in the doorway, and she could hear his breathing, feel the heat emanating from his flesh. It was hot in the room, wonderfully warm.

And then she noticed the clothes on the floor. His jeans and T-shirt lay in a haphazard pile, which could mean one of two things. Either he'd changed his clothes—and she knew all their extra clothes had burned with the house—or he was lying on the bed, wearing nothing but his hot, smooth skin.

The old springs creaked in the night, and she knew he was awake. "Just as well you can't see me," he murmured, his voice low and beguiling.

"Why?"

"You'd blush."

She could feel color suffuse her face. "I have pale skin," she protested.

She could feel his silence. Feel his longing. Feel him burning for her. As she burned for him.

"Denial is not just a river in Egypt," he murmured, and unbelieving she heard the next words, the ones she'd longed for, in his mind.

She couldn't see him, so she simply closed her eyes. And reaching down, she pulled her T-shirt over her head and sent it sailing onto the floor, where it landed beside his.

The jeans came next. She was wearing plain white cotton bikini panties, and she stripped those off, as well, so that she was standing in the moonlit darkness, naked, vulnerable.

She knew he watched her—she could feel his eyes on her body like a caress, running down her long legs, up over her stomach, cupping her breasts. She tilted her head back, reveling in the heat of his gaze, and her shoulder-length hair trailed down her back. When she looked at the bed again there was a faint, possessive smile on her face.

"You're an idiot, Dr. Crompton," she said, moving toward the sagging mattress.

"Why do you say that, Molloy?" He sounded merely curious, but the husky note in his voice betrayed his reaction to her as surely as the sight of him would have.

She stopped beside the bed, feeling the luscious heat wash over her. "Because you're afraid of the best thing that ever happened to you."

"I don't..." he began, but she leaned down, unerringly, putting her hand against his unseen mouth.

"Shut up, Daniel," she said kindly. "I'll take care of things." And she put her mouth where her hand had been.

His mouth was hot, damp, open for her. She threaded her hands through his long hair, and she could feel the stubble of his beard. He hadn't shaved all day—Osborn had woken them out of an exhausted sleep, and they'd been running so long that she hadn't even noticed.

She liked the roughness of his cheeks. She drew her mouth away and rubbed her face against his unseen one, still feeling his beard against her tender skin. She was kneeling on the bed beside him, and she felt his hands slide around her waist, hot against her cool skin, and she leaned against him, absorbing the feel of him, the warmth of him, the strength of him.

He tried to tug her down beside him, beneath him, but she held back. "Not this time," she murmured.

"What do you mean?"

"I mean that I've never had the chance to make love to an invisible man in my life. It seems likely that you're going to be spending a lot of time in that condition, and I intend to be spending a lot of time with you. I'd better get used to it."

She let her hands trail down the sides of his face, exploring the feel of him, and let them rest on his bare shoulders.

She let her eyes drift closed. She'd never realized how intensely erotic it could be, touching without seeing. She learned him, the shape and texture of him, as she'd never learned a man before. With only her other senses available, with taste and touch and smell, she had to concentrate on the slightest clues. The pebbled hardness of his flat male nipples, the faint, rasping sound of his breath as she trailed her mouth across his stomach, the tension in his skin, his hands, as he forced himself to let her discover him. When he lay back on the bare mattress, she heard the shift of the springs beneath him. She slid her hands up, to discover he'd wrapped his own strong hands around the iron bedstead. She could feel the pressure, the strength in them, and she smiled, opening her eyes to stare down into nothingness.

"You're showing wonderful restraint," she murmured approvingly, leaning forward to brush a kiss against his mouth. She missed her target, landing instead on his chin, but he moved, swiftly, unerringly, his mouth meeting hers, and she could taste his hunger, taste his need.

"Stay like that," she whispered, learning him with her mouth, letting her lips taste and nibble their way down his smooth, hot chest, past his stomach and the faint roughness of hair. She put her hands around him, gently, and he groaned, and she heard the creak of the springs as he arched beneath her.

He was huge, and hard, and damp for her. He didn't need to say a word—she knew what he wanted, she could hear his desperate longing in his mind, and it matched her own. She leaned down and put her mouth on him, taking him deep inside, her hands clutching his hips.

He didn't touch her, and she knew why. If he touched her, he'd take over, and he knew she needed to do this. Needed to take control, to learn him, without fear of the consequences. She needed to do just what she wanted, and she needed him to lie back and let her.

He was shaking. She could feel the trembling in his body, and it matched her own. She wanted him this way, she wanted him every way there was, but she could hear his protest. And then he spoke, his voice raw and strained in the empty darkness.

"Not without you," he said, and she knew he loved her.

Reluctantly she pulled away, and she could feel his silent cry of pain. And then she slid up, over him, and as she slowly sank down she could feel the iron-hard tension in every muscle in his body, as he controlled his need to surge into her.

He waited until she'd taken him fully. Waited until she leaned forward, her breasts against his hot chest, her hands sliding up his outstretched arms to cover his hands as they clutched the iron railing. He waited while she moved, awkwardly at first, unsure, and then suddenly she was fluid, light and darkness, heat and desire, taking him, owning him, and he was trembling, shaking apart beneath her, and she was trembling, shaking apart, and then the world exploded. She screamed, unable to stop herself, and she was lost, as he finally began to move, thrusting up into her, taking her, filling her with his heat, his seed, his life.

She didn't want to open her eyes. She could still feel his heart pounding beneath hers, feel the strangled rasp of his breathing as it stirred her hair, still feel him within her body. His hands loosened their fierce hold of the iron bedstead and turned beneath hers, clasping hers, and she wanted to weep at the beauty of it. If she opened her eyes reality would intrude. For now, there were only the two of them, alone in the universe.

SHE MUST HAVE DOZED. She awoke with the room in pitch-blackness, the moon gone behind dark, scudding clouds. Unseen hands were turning her, tucking her next to a fiery body, and she breathed a sigh of pure contentment as his hands pulled her closer.

He leaned forward, his mouth brushing her ear, and she waited for his words of love. "Where are you in your menstrual cycle?" he asked endearingly.

She shoved at him. "Do you have to be quite so practical?"

"So sue me. I'm a scientist."

"Not, however, a biologist," she pointed out, glad the darkness hid the blush she knew suffused her face.

"I had a fair amount of pre-med. I didn't use any protection. I'm no longer worried about other side-effects, but an unplanned pregnancy is still a concern."

"What other side-effects?" she asked warily.

"I've been exposed to something quite extraordinary, something that's changed my body chemistry. It didn't seem a wise idea to introduce any fluids into your body without checking."

"How romantic," she murmured sarcastically. "What makes you think it's all right now?"

"I checked."

"How'd you manage that?"

She didn't have to see him to recognize the wicked grin in his voice. "I just needed to check a sample under the microscope. Easy enough to procure one. I just closed my eyes and thought of you."

She didn't know whether to hit him or kiss him. He was absolutely the most damnable, frustrating, erotic, endearing man on the face of the planet. Even if she was unable to see him for too much of the time.

She let herself relax against him, sliding into his warmth. "They think we're dead, you know. It was on the television news."

He didn't seem surprised. "I heard it on the car radio while you slept."

"I called Uncle Vinnie and asked him to let your parents know you were all right...."

"You did what?"

He pulled away from her, sitting up in the darkness, and there was no missing the anger in his unseen body, any more than she could miss the faint red glow in his eyes.

She stared in his direction, fascinated. "I can see your eyes glowing," she murmured.

"The hell with my eyes! Why did you call him?"

"Don't get into such a swivet. You may not care what people think, but I wasn't about to have them holding a memorial service for me. I have people who love me. I figure even you do, though it's hard to imagine. I expect your parents might experience a pang or two if they thought their only child had burned up in a forest fire." Her voice was caustic.

"They would have survived a couple of days thinking that. They're pragmatic people."

"No one's pragmatic enough to accept the loss of their child."

"Maybe. But did you stop and think about what your little good deed for the day might have done?"

"They couldn't trace the call, if that's what you're worried about. I used Osborn's cellular phone—there's no way they could tap it."

"You'd be surprised at what they can do. But they wouldn't have to tap Osborn's phone. They just have to tap the phones of people you'd be likely to call. My parents would have been first on the list. Hell and damnation!"

"I didn't even talk to them. I just told Vinnie to call, and I didn't give him any specific information, apart from telling him we were still alive and Osborn was dead. We'll be perfectly safe."

"I'm not worried about us. I'm worried about my parents. About your damned Uncle Vinnie, for that matter. If they know we care enough to be in touch with them, they'll use them for bargaining chips. And I don't think they're about to let anybody walk away from this mess."

"Oh, God," Suzanna murmured. "Daniel, I'm sorry."

There was a stunned silence. "And here I thought supersensitive hearing was part of my metamorphosis. Suzanna Molloy is not a girl to say she's sorry."

"Don't call me *girl*," she said miserably in token protest.

She felt his hand reach up under her hair and stroke her face gently. "They'll be all right, Molloy. We'll get the bad guys. I'm not about to let them get away with this."

"But there are so many of them," she said.

"Yeah, but you forget. I'm Cinderman, crusader for truth and justice. With my faithful companion, Suzanna the mind-reading swami, beside me, there's no way the armies of evil will triumph."

"This isn't a comic book, Daniel," she said sternly.

"Life's a comic book, Molloy. The sooner you realize that, the better off you'll be."

She stared up at him. The moon had reappeared from behind the clouds, and she could see his outline in the darkness. "It must be after eight," she said.

"It is. I changed back while you were sleeping." He reached over and turned on the light, and she closed her eyes against the brightness. "We've got to get moving, swami," he muttered. "We don't have any time to waste."

She scrambled for her clothes on the far side of the bed, yanking her T-shirt over her head in belated embarrassment. It had been easy enough to be a wanton in the dark, with no visible witness. The memory of what they'd done was suddenly overwhelming.

Daniel was standing in the middle of the room, motionless, staring past her. He'd pulled on his jeans, and there was a bemused expression on his face.

"What are you staring at?" she demanded.

"The bed."

She didn't know what she'd expected. She was almost afraid to look. When she turned to follow his gaze, she was momentarily breathless.

The sturdy iron bedstead had been bent like an old wire coat hanger.

She remembered her hands on his in the darkness, clutching those heavy iron bars. "Goodness," she said quietly.

"Or as Mae West once said, 'Goodness has nothing to do with it,'" he replied. "Get your clothes on, Suzanna. You're far too distracting that way, and we have work to do."

She was tempted to point out just how distracting he was, then thought better of it. "Where are we going?"

"To get the bad guys, Suzanna. Before they get us."

IF HE'D HAD THE CHOICE, Daniel thought, he would have clipped Ms. Suzanna Molloy on the chin and left her safely tied up back at the deserted old house. But he didn't have the choice. She knew half the things he was thinking—there'd be no way he could sneak up on her without her guessing. And he had no guarantee she'd be any safer back there. At least, with him, she had supernatural powers on her side. For some reason he didn't think twenty-twenty vision and the ability to read certain thoughts were going to be enough to protect her from people like Armstead and his crew of disenchanted ex-Green Berets.

There was never any doubt in his mind where he'd find Armstead. He'd be at Beebe, waiting for him to come in. They understood each other in ways far more direct than Suzanna's swami act. They were too much alike. Megalomaniacs, with only one purpose. For Armstead, it was the control of the world with his own particular agenda. For Daniel, it was the quest for knowledge.

Except that he had another purpose, one that had sneaked up on him when he wasn't looking. Another interest, one he was as passionately devoted to as he was to bi-level molecular transfer. And that was Suzanna Molloy.

One thing was certain—if they were going to stay together, he was going to have to figure out a way to shield his thoughts from her. He didn't fancy spending the rest of his life with a mental voyeur in his bed.

But he didn't fancy spending the rest of his life without her, either.

There'd be time enough for dealing with that later. Assuming there was a later. For now he had to concentrate on bringing Armstead and his army of creeps down. There was simply too damned much at stake.

The huge white headquarters of Beebe Control Systems International looked deserted when he drove Osborn's Jaguar into the empty parking lot, but Daniel wasn't fooled for a moment. They were there, behind those darkened windows, waiting for him. He only hoped Cinderman was ready for them.

Suzanna slid out of the car and came to stand beside him. He'd parked in front of the entrance, taking a cool sip of defiance in leaving the front tires on the handicapped accessible walkway that had never seen anyone in a wheelchair. There was a cool breeze, one that he barely felt with his heated skin, but it blew Suzanna's hair back against his shoulder, and he caught the faint trace of her shampoo. He wanted to stop right then and there, drag her back to the Jaguar and push her down onto the back seat.

He simply took her hand, running his thumb over her long, strong fingers. "I can't persuade you to run away and hide, can I?" he asked, almost absently.

"No."

He glanced down at her. "I have a funny feeling about tonight."

He saw the flicker of sheer panic in her eyes, saw her swiftly control it. "Funny like what?"

"Funny like I'm not going to walk out of there alive."

She didn't make a sound, but he could hear the sudden panicked lurch of her heart. "In that case, it doesn't really matter whether I come with you or not," she observed in a deceptive drawl. "You don't have any funny feelings that I'm not going to make it, do you?"

"No."

"Then I'll come with you," she said firmly. "Two against an army is better than one."

"I don't want you doing anything foolish."

"Like what?"

"Like making any dramatic gestures to save me if things get out of control. I want you to promise me."

"Promise you what?"

"That you'll do as I say. That you'll trust my judgment."

She turned and stared at him, and he thought he could see the faint glimmer of tears in her perfect eyes. "Are you crazy, Daniel? Me, trust your judgment? Give me a good reason."

"Because I don't want you to die, too."

She was silent. And then she rallied, as he knew she would, and he found it in him to grin. "Why not?" she demanded.

"Read my mind," he whispered, leaning down and brushing his lips against hers.

He felt the shock that went through her, the yearning. And then he set her away, staring up at the monstrous edifice that housed Armstead and his goons and the fruits of his own work for the last five years. The secrets to bi-level molecular transfer.

"No," she said, following his gaze. "You can't do it."

He didn't bother denying it. "Why not? Just a stare, a blink, a scrunch of my nose and this place will be a pile of cinders. Those are the bad guys inside, Molloy. Tell me why I should give them a chance to get us first."

"Because we're the good guys."

He considered it for a moment. "The problem with you, Molloy," he drawled, "is that you're usually right. Come on."

She held back, just for a moment. "How are we going to get in?"

"I expect they've unlocked the door for us. There'll be a welcoming party. Are you sure you don't want to run while you still have the chance?"

"Do you?"

"Not on your life."

"Then I'm coming with you."

Chapter Seventeen

"We expected you earlier, Dr. Crompton." The man stepped out of the shadows in the cavernous, deserted hallway, and Daniel didn't need any light to identify him.

"I try not to be predictable, Cole," he said easily. "I don't think you met Suzanna when we were here earlier. Suzanna, this is General Armstead's favorite gofer. Cole Slaughter."

"Great name," Suzanna muttered, glancing at Slaughter's camouflage fatigues and blunt, brutal face.

He didn't even register her presence. "General Armstead is awaiting your presence, sir," he said, the essence of military politeness.

"I'm sure he is," Daniel drawled. "Are you going to escort us, or shall we find him ourselves?"

"He wasn't expecting Ms. Molloy."

"If you know her last name, then you must have had a fairly good idea she'd be with me. She stays with me, Slaughter. Got that?"

"Yes, sir. If you'll follow me." He turned, leading the way through the shadowy hallway, and Daniel reached out his hand for Suzanna's, wondering if she'd take it, or if she'd be determined to prove how tough she still was.

A moment later her hand was tucked into his, holding tightly. He could feel the chill in her flesh—magnified because he was so hot. He wished there was some way to keep her out of this mess, but she was already in it up to her ears. His best chance of keeping her safe was keeping her with him, no matter what they ended up confronting.

"There you are." General Armstead rose from his thronelike seat at the end of the huge walnut table. He'd taken up residence in the boardroom, and he looked like a squat, evil spider. He was wearing a combat uniform not unlike Slaughter's—an odd choice for a retired soldier. But then, the truth was, Armstead was far from retired.

"Sorry to keep you waiting," Daniel murmured, still holding Suzanna's hand tightly. "Where are the rest of your little soldier boys? Surely you don't think you can rule the world with an army of one Robocop?"

Slaughter made a growling noise in the back of his throat, but he didn't move. He remained standing to one side, awaiting orders.

Armstead took a step toward them, a genial expression on his face. "But I don't need an army, son. It's better to keep your team down to the bare minimum— less fuss, less danger of betrayal. Slaughter here has been with me since Nam. He was just a boy then—fifteen—but big for his age. He already had a real gift back then. One he's honed."

"I can imagine," Daniel said dryly.

"By the way, where's Osborn? I sent him to get you. That, or dispose of you. Am I to assume, since you arrived here in his car, that he didn't make it back from Oregon?"

"You can assume all you like. At least *part* of that news story you fed the press was correct."

"Dear me," Armstead said, not the slightest bit disturbed. "Slaughter, I'll let you be the one to console his wife. The woman's a bit too hungry for me."

"Yes, sir," said Slaughter, sounding more and more like a robot.

"And now, my dear Dr. Crompton, I'm afraid we've wasted far too much time playing games. You know what I want. Beebe has paid for it, paid you extravagant sums of money, along with footing your research. It's time for the results."

"What if I told you I didn't have any results? That it had all been a waste?"

"I wouldn't believe you," Armstead said simply. "I'd be willing to bet you all that money you have squirreled away in some Swiss bank account that you possess the secret that could rule the universe. And I want that secret, Daniel. I have no intention of waiting any longer. This whole organization has already been compromised. With Osborn dead, we'll be facing some unpleasant questions. I'll find a good use for your research, my boy. After all, I paid for it."

"You and your rich, paranoid cronies." Daniel shrugged. "You stole my notes. You know as much as I do."

"Ah, yes, those notes. Very cryptic of you. We almost overlooked that disk when we searched your apartment.

Fortunately Slaughter pointed out that you were hardly the man to own a Neil Diamond CD. And there wasn't even a stereo in your condo."

Daniel glanced over at the enigmatic Slaughter. "All this, and brains too, Cole? Will wonders never cease."

Again that low, warning growl. "I wouldn't, if I were you, Crompton," Armstead said gently. "Major Slaughter doesn't possess much of a sense of humor. And he's experienced enough to know who to take it out on. I don't think you'd enjoy seeing what a man with Slaughter's talent would do with Ms. Molloy."

Daniel's hand tightened automatically around Suzanna's, and it was sheer force of will that kept him from imagining exactly what kind of things Slaughter might do. Suzanna was entirely capable of reading his thoughts, and if she wasn't terrified already, it would send her over the edge.

"So tell me what you want, Armstead," Daniel said with deceptive calm. "You have my notes. Surely Beebe can afford to pay a competent scientist to decipher them, to replicate my experiments."

"We've already had a competent scientist do just that. Unfortunately, Dr. Jackson showed an unfortunate level of greed. That's the problem with working within an organization. You're only as strong as your weakest link. That's why I decided to take Slaughter and Osborn on as partners in our own little enterprise, and not worry about the rest of Beebe's infrastructure. You can never be sure of anyone's limits. I would have had Jackson join us, too, if he hadn't proven so acquisitive."

"Is that why you killed him?"

"Actually, Slaughter and Osborn did the honors. Slaughter finished him up, but not before he had Jackson explain exactly what bi-level molecular transfer is."

Daniel didn't even blink. "And what does he think it is?"

"Alchemy." It was a little more than a groan from Slaughter, but not much.

Daniel managed a wintry smile. "That's succinct."

"I want the formula," Armstead said.

"You have it."

"You know as well as I do that it's missing one crucial piece. I want to know where that is."

"Someplace where you'll never find it," Daniel replied.

"Son," Armstead said heavily, "don't make me do this."

"I'm not your son," Daniel said. "And I'm not one of your damned Robocops. You're not getting it out of me—you'll have to kill me first."

Armstead simply shook his grizzled gray head. "I'm afraid, dear boy," he murmured, "that's hardly a threat. We were going to kill you, anyway. We'll just start with Ms. Molloy. And it will be very, very painful. Slaughter."

"Keep your hands off her," Crompton snarled, enraged, but he didn't move fast enough. Slaughter had already spun her away, and if Daniel had made the mistake of holding on, her wrist would have been crushed.

Suzanna didn't say a word. She just looked at him, silent, horrified, and Slaughter pulled her back against his uniformed body, a slender, professional-looking knife at the delicate column of her throat.

"I think we're at a standoff," Armstead announced pleasantly. "Do you feel like being more cooperative, Dr. Crompton? Or do you want to see how much blood it will take to soak through that offensive T-shirt? Where is the missing piece of information?"

He didn't hesitate any longer. "In my brain. And if you don't get away from her, right now, you're never going to find out the answer."

"Dear me," the general murmured. "That's quite unfortunate. I wonder, Slaughter, whether we ought to call his bluff?"

"You needn't worry, sir. I can finish with this one and then get what you want out of the doctor," Slaughter said confidently, and the knife glittered in the low light like the caress of a silver-fingered butcher. "He's not going to be able to stand up to me."

"You'd be surprised, Slaughter," Armstead said, leaning back against the table. "The good doctor has had a surprising amount of training. As a matter of fact, I was one of the ones who approved it, back before I retired. With an asset like his mind, we didn't want to take any risks. He'd be harder to crack than you think. Let the girl go."

"Don't," Suzanna said, her voice strangled against the pressure of the knife, "call me *girl*." And she slammed her elbow backward into Slaughter's unprotected belly.

He doubled over in shock, and she kicked back, directly into his groin. In a few seconds he was writhing on the floor, shrieking with pain, the knife skittering across the thick carpeted floor.

She leapt for Daniel, but Armstead's voice stopped her. "Don't move," he said. He had a gun trained on her, and it was a very large, very nasty-looking one.

"Not again," she said wearily. "Aren't you men tired of playing spies?"

Armstead's smile was a travesty. "I'm going to shoot you in the knee, Ms. Molloy. If Dr. Crompton doesn't start talking, I'll shoot you in the other knee. And then I'll work my way upward. This gun has eight bullets, and they're large ones. I can do a great deal of damage, cause a great deal of pain. I do, however, promise that the final one will go in your brain."

"Kind of you," she said faintly. She glanced at Daniel. "I think you should know, Daniel, that he's really going to do it. You have no choice."

He accepted the message as gospel. There was no way out—Suzanna had heard Armstead's thoughts and knew just how bad they were. If he didn't stop him, the one way he could, then Suzanna would be dead.

Armstead cocked the gun and pointed it, not at Suzanna's knee, but directly toward her belly. Slaughter was already struggling upward, and Daniel had less than a second to decide.

He didn't decide. He acted. Armstead fired the gun, Daniel shoved Suzanna to the floor, and in the millisecond before Armstead could fire again, he was a human torch.

He didn't even have time to scream.

Suzanna was in his arms, her face hidden against his chest, before the ash and cinder collapsed in a heap on the floor, the charcoaled remains of General Jack Armstead.

"Oh, my God," Slaughter moaned in horror. He'd managed to struggle to his feet, but his color was still white from pain and shock. "I'm outta here," he muttered. And he took off at a dead run, before Daniel could move.

"Let's get out of here," he said, keeping her face turned away from what little was left of Armstead. He steered her out the door, and she went, shaking slightly, quiet, as docile as he'd ever seen her.

By the time they reached the front lobby there was no sign of Slaughter, and Daniel had no doubt he was gone for good. "Damn," he said, and Suzanna raised her head, following his gaze.

Bright white headlights were spearing their way across the darkened parking lot, pulling to a stop inches away from the abandoned Jaguar. She could see the shape of the familiar white Cadillac, and she knew with crushing certainty just who had arrived to rescue her.

"It's Uncle Vinnie," she said, watching as he approached the front entrance, flanked by Guido and Vito, his two huge nephews who were probably no more his nephews that she was his niece.

Daniel released her. "Go talk to him," he said smoothly. "Get him away from here."

She started to move, then halted, turning back to stare at him. "What about you?"

"I have to see to a few things."

"You're not going after Slaughter, are you?"

"No. He's lost Armstead, and he has to live with his own panic. That's the worst punishment for a killing machine like him. He's ruined."

"Then what are you going back for?"

"I have to make sure the research is destroyed. I don't want any trace of bi-level molecular transfer left."

"Why?" she protested. "After all your work..."

"It's too dangerous. There are too many men like Osborn and Armstead. Men who wouldn't think of using me, of using you to get to me. You won't be safe—hell, the world won't be safe—until it's gone."

She didn't move. Guido was holding the door for Uncle Vinnie, but she didn't even glance their way. "You can't," she said. "You can't get rid of all of it. Part of it's in your brain. You can't..."

"Yes," he said, very gently. "I can. Take her with you, Uncle Vinnie. Don't let her back in this place."

"No!" Suzanna shrieked, but Vinnie was quick to move. Vito caught her up in his burly arms, and she was no match for him. He carried her out of the building, Guido following, as she screamed and cried, shouting curses at his head.

Vinnie looked up at Daniel. "You must be Dr. Crompton," he said.

"And you're Uncle Vinnie."

Vinnie smiled faintly. "She loves you."

"I know. You'll see to her, won't you? This won't be easy for her."

"You have no choice?" he asked delicately.

Daniel simply shook his head, a cynical smile on his face. "I'm America's secret weapon, remember? No one knows better than me that there's no choice. As long as the information in my brain survives, she won't be safe. And I can think of only one way to get rid of this place, and my memory. It won't take long."

Vinnie's eyes were huge and sad. "I'll go to her."

Daniel watched him turn and head toward the door. In the distance he could see Suzanna still struggling as the nephews tried to strong-arm her into the waiting Cadillac. "Tell her—" he said, and then stopped himself.

"Tell her what?" Vinnie asked.

Daniel shook his head. "Never mind. She'll know."

SHE COULD NO LONGER scream. Her voice was gone, silenced. She could no longer cry. Her tears had dried up. She could only sit there, trapped in the back seat of Vinnie's Cadillac, and shake.

"I'm sorry it had to be this way," Vinnie said from the front seat as Guido started the car. Vito sat beside her, his hamlike hand a manacle across her wrist, but she was beyond struggling. She accepted defeat, and loss, and despair.

She looked up, and a shaft of flame shot through the roof, spearing toward the sky. Another followed, a bright white fireball, and within seconds the huge building was in flames.

Guido stopped the car, staring in amazement at the conflagration, and even Vinnie was awed. "What in God's name did he do?" he gasped.

Suzanna watched, dry-eyed, empty-hearted. And then she heard him. Heard the words, clear and true, through the heat and smoke of the fiery inferno. *I love you, Molloy.*

She could make a sound after all. It was a low, keening whimper, like an animal in pain, as she felt her heart torn out and incinerated. They sat in the car and watched as the building collapsed in a pile of blazing ash.

"That couldn't have happened," Vinnie muttered. "Things can't burn that quickly. A bomb, maybe, but the fire should have lasted. . . ."

Guido was murmuring, and it took Suzanna a moment to realize it was the Latin prayers he'd learned in his youth, as he stared up at the remnants of the huge building with superstitious horror.

"We have to get out of here. The fire department's gonna show up, and we don't want to be here when they start asking their questions," Vinnie announced, his voice still shaken. "Get moving, Guido."

Guido just stared, unable to move. Vito was equally shocked, craning his neck to peer out the window, releasing his grip on Suzanna. She stared out the smoked window, into the conflagration.

And then she saw movement.

"Stop the car," she screamed, her voice a raw travesty.

"Keep driving," Vinnie ordered. "I can hear the sirens already."

Guido kept driving. Suzanna twisted the door handle and rolled out, moving too fast for Vito to stop her.

She hit the ground running, racing across the deserted parking lot toward the glowing remains of the huge building. Osborn's Jaguar had disappeared in the flames, and nothing was left standing of Daniel's funeral pyre.

And then she saw movement again. She heard the fire-engine sirens and saw the reflection of the flashing lights in the distance as they raced toward the ruins, but she ignored them, focusing instead on the smoldering debris. The white Cadillac started to drive off, leaving her in the predawn darkness.

The charred remains shifted, moving once more, and the shadow grew. She stood there alone, sobbing, as his shape took form, and Daniel Crompton walked out of the fire, and into her arms.

The Cadillac screeched up beside them, the door opened, and Vinnie pulled them in. "For God's sake, let's go," he yelled, and this time Guido drove as he'd been trained to do, out of sight before the first fire engine pulled up to the charred remains of Beebe Control Systems International.

Vito kept out of her way as she held Daniel tightly in her arms. His eyes were closed, his breathing hoarse, and she clutched him, murmuring over and over again, soothing words, crazy words, telling him she hated him, she'd kill him, she loved him, she'd kill him.

He smiled against her face, not opening his eyes, and her tears washed some of the soot from his face. "Hush," he said finally, pulling her tight against him. "It's over."

"No, it's not," she wept in a raw voice, rocking him back and forth. "It will never be over. I hate you, I hate you..."

"It's over," he said again, and she pressed her face against his cool skin, trembling.

"Where do you want me to drive, Uncle Vinnie?" Guido asked. "You want to go home now?"

"What time is it?" Vinnie asked absently.

"A little after seven. We could stop for breakfast at Mama Lucia's. A nice omelet, some *cafe latte*. We can bring some out for the doc and Ms. Molloy."

Suzanna held herself very still. "What time did you say it was?"

"After seven. It's been a long night, *cara*," Vinnie murmured. "But it's morning now. A new day. A new beginning." The car pulled up in front of a cheery-looking trattoria on the outskirts of Santa Cristina. "You want anything to eat?"

"She always does," Daniel murmured faintly. "Just bring her out something with cholesterol."

"And you, my boy?"

"Something hot. I've got a chill."

She waited until they were alone in the back seat. "Your skin is cool," she said.

"And I feel weak as a kitten," he added. "And best of all, I can't remember what I've been working on for the past two years."

"What do you mean?"

"Just that. My notes were wiped out in the fire, and I can't even begin to remember where I started. I guess I'll have to find something new to work on. Maybe cold fusion."

She held herself very still. "Sure, try something easy for a change."

He smiled up at her, then shifted until he lay with his head in her lap. "You'd better marry me," he said, closing his eyes again.

"Another one of your romantic overtures, Dr. Crompton?"

"Just trying to tell you what to do, Molloy. I need help rebuilding the place in Oregon. Though this time maybe we'll make it a little larger. I want a bigger lab if I'm going to work there full-time, and you'll probably want an office of your own."

"Not to mention a better kitchen. And a television, and a satellite dish. And while you're at it, why don't you tell me what I'm supposed to do out there at the back of beyond?" she demanded in the raw travesty that once was her voice.

He eyed her. "I thought you liked it there. Don't you have any ideas?"

"A number of them. I think I'll write science fiction. I take it money isn't a problem?"

"The late Beebe Control Systems International paid me huge amounts of their ill-gotten gains. We'll be more than comfortable."

"Then I think I'll write a series of novels about the Invisible Man."

He groaned, reached up, pulled her head down and kissed her. His mouth was cool and delicious. "I love you," he said.

"I know. I heard."

He kissed her again, a little more lingering, a little deeper. "It's gone, you know. Everything vanished in that inferno. Cinderman died in the fire."

"Do you mind?"

"Not at all. Though it's going to give you an unfair advantage."

"Hey, I'll need all the advantages I can get to keep up with you and whatever little geniuses you happen to beget." She looked down at him, love in her eyes, in her heart, in her ruined voice.

"We'll have to make the place even bigger."

"We'll have time."

He looked up at her, for a moment sweetly vulnerable. "I really did forget everything," he murmured.

"Of course you did," she said, looking into his mind, understanding him very well. "And you're going to have lots of fun playing with that green slime you brought out of the fire."

He stared at her for a moment, and then a wry smile lit his face. "I'm never going to be able to lie to you."

"Accept it. I'm your destiny, Cinderman, your ball and chain. There's no way you'll escape me."

"Dear girl," he said faintly, "I wouldn't think of it."

"Don't," she said, "call me *girl*." And she leaned down to kiss him again, as his hand twined in her hair, and there was no more need for words.

Epilogue

The house perched on the edge of the cliff was a magical house, filled with light and laughter, love and warmth. Suzanna sat barefoot in the garden, hands folded neatly on her pregnant belly, wearing a T-shirt that read She Who Rocks the Cradle Rules the World—Watch Out! She watched the twins argue amicably enough, used to it by now. Albert Einstein Molloy Crompton had decided that Charles Dickens was a sexist pig, albeit a good storyteller, but he much preferred Jane Austen and Georgette Heyer, like his father. His sister, Marie Curie Molloy Crompton, insisted that he ought to be paying more attention to the writings of his namesake than to stories, even if their mother made a fairly good living writing them.

They were both five years old.

She smiled fondly. This was an old battle, without any particular rancor, and it had been going on since they were three. "Where's your father, Marie?" she asked, feeling the baby kick. At least there was only one this time. Two, even with Daniel's fascinated assistance, was a little more challenge than she felt like facing again.

"Can't you listen for him?" Albert asked, used to her odd powers.

"He's keeping me out," Suzanna said. "Singing those stupid songs so I can't eavesdrop."

"He says you're a voyeur," Marie said cheerfully.

"I'm just curious— Oh, my God!" The explosion rocked the ground, glass shattered, and a billow of pure white smoke shot out the broken window of the lab. She struggled awkwardly to her feet, holding her belly, and ran toward the house.

She barreled straight into something, and strong arms reached out to catch her.

"You'll never guess what I've discovered," Daniel's disembodied voice announced with disgusting cheer.

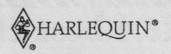

HARLEQUIN®

MARRIAGE *By Design*

Harlequin proudly presents four stories about *convenient* but not *conventional* reasons for marriage:

- ◆ To save your godchildren from a "wicked stepmother"

- ◆ To help out your eccentric aunt — and her sexy business partner

- ◆ To bring an old man happiness by making him a grandfather

- ◆ To escape from a ghostly existence and become a real woman

Marriage By Design — four brand-new stories by four of Harlequin's most popular authors:

CATHY GILLEN THACKER
JASMINE CRESSWELL
GLENDA SANDERS
MARGARET CHITTENDEN

Don't miss this exciting collection of stories about marriages of convenience. Available in April, wherever Harlequin books are sold.

MBD94

Take 4 bestselling love stories FREE

Plus get a FREE surprise gift!

Special Limited-time Offer

Mail to Harlequin Reader Service®

> P.O. Box 609
> Fort Erie, Ontario
> L2A 5X3

YES! Please send me 4 free Harlequin American Romance® novels and my free surprise gift. Then send me 4 brand-new novels every month, which I will receive months before they appear in bookstores. Bill me at the low price of $2.96 each plus 25¢ delivery and GST*. That's the complete price and— compared to the cover prices of $3.50 each—quite a bargain! I understand that accepting the books and gift places me under no obligation ever to buy any books. I can always return a shipment and cancel at any time. Even if I never buy another book from Harlequin, the 4 free books and the surprise gift are mine to keep forever.

354 BPA AJJQ

Name	(PLEASE PRINT)	
Address	Apt. No.	
City	Province	Postal Code

This offer is limited to one order per household and not valid to present Harlequin American Romance® subscribers. *Terms and prices are subject to change without notice.
Canadian residents will be charged applicable provincial taxes and GST.

CAMER-94R   ©1990 Harlequin Enterprises Limited

HARLEQUIN®

Don't miss these Harlequin favorites by some of our most distin-
guished authors!
And now, you can receive a discount by ordering two or more titles!

HT#25409	THE NIGHT IN SHINING ARMOR by JoAnn Ross	$2.99	☐
HT#25471	LOVESTORM by JoAnn Ross	$2.99	☐
HP#11463	THE WEDDING by Emma Darcy	$2.89	☐
HP#11592	THE LAST GRAND PASSION by Emma Darcy	$2.99	☐
HR#03188	DOUBLY DELICIOUS by Emma Goldrick	$2.89	☐
HR#03248	SAFE IN MY HEART by Leigh Michaels	$2.89	☐
HS#70464	CHILDREN OF THE HEART by Sally Garrett	$3.25	☐
HS#70524	STRING OF MIRACLES by Sally Garrett	$3.39	☐
HS#70500	THE SILENCE OF MIDNIGHT by Karen Young	$3.39	☐
HI#22178	SCHOOL FOR SPIES by Vickie York	$2.79	☐
HI#22212	DANGEROUS VINTAGE by Laura Pender	$2.89	☐
HI#22219	TORCH JOB by Patricia Rosemoor	$2.89	☐
HAR#16459	MACKENZIE'S BABY by Anne McAllister	$3.39	☐
HAR#16466	A COWBOY FOR CHRISTMAS by Anne McAllister	$3.39	☐
HAR#16462	THE PIRATE AND HIS LADY by Margaret St. George	$3.39	☐
HAR#16477	THE LAST REAL MAN by Rebecca Flanders	$3.39	☐
HH#28704	A CORNER OF HEAVEN by Theresa Michaels	$3.99	☐
HH#28707	LIGHT ON THE MOUNTAIN by Maura Seger	$3.99	☐

Harlequin Promotional Titles

#83247	YESTERDAY COMES TOMORROW by Rebecca Flanders	$4.99	☐
#83257	MY VALENTINE 1993	$4.99	☐
	(short-story collection featuring Anne Stuart, Judith Arnold, Anne McAllister, Linda Randall Wisdom)		

(limited quantities available on certain titles)

	AMOUNT	$
DEDUCT:	10% DISCOUNT FOR 2+ BOOKS	$
ADD:	POSTAGE & HANDLING	$
	($1.00 for one book, 50¢ for each additional)	
	APPLICABLE TAXES*	$ _____
	TOTAL PAYABLE	$ _____
	(check or money order—please do not send cash)	

To order, complete this form and send it, along with a check or money order for the
total above, payable to Harlequin Books, to: **In the U.S.:** 3010 Walden Avenue,
P.O. Box 9047, Buffalo, NY 14269-9047; **In Canada:** P.O. Box 613, Fort Erie, Ontario,
L2A 5X3.

Name: _____

Address: _____ City: _____

State/Prov.: _____ Zip/Postal Code: _____

*New York residents remit applicable sales taxes.
Canadian residents remit applicable GST and provincial taxes.

HBACK-JM

When the only time you have for yourself is...

Spring into spring—by giving yourself a March Break! Take a few *stolen moments* and treat yourself to a Great Escape. Relax with one of our brand-new stories (or with all six!).

Each STOLEN MOMENTS title in our Great Escapes collection is a complete and never-before-published *short* novel. These contemporary romances are 96 pages long—the perfect length for the busy woman of the nineties!

Look for Great Escapes in our Stolen Moments display this March!

SIZZLE by Jennifer Crusie
ANNIVERSARY WALTZ
by Anne Marie Duquette
MAGGIE AND HER COLONEL
by Merline Lovelace
PRAIRIE SUMMER by Alina Roberts
THE SUGAR CUP by Annie Sims
LOVE ME NOT by Barbara Stewart

Wherever Harlequin and Silhouette books are sold.

HARLEQUIN®

A M E R I C A N ◆ R O M A N C E □

Meet four of the most mysterious, magical men in

MORE
THAN
MEN

These men are more than tall, dark and handsome. They have extraordinary powers that make them "more than men." But whether they are able to grant you three wishes, communicate with dolphins or live forever, make no mistake—their greatest, most extraordinary power is of seduction.

Make a date with all these MORE THAN MEN:

#501	A WISH...AND A KISS by Margaret St. George	$3.50	☐
#509	NEPTUNE'S BRIDE by Anne Marie Duquette	$3.50	☐
#517	FOREVER ALWAYS by Rebecca Flanders	$3.50	☐
#525	CINDERMAN by Anne Stuart	$3.50	☐

(limited quantities available on certain titles)

TOTAL AMOUNT	$
POSTAGE & HANDLING	$
($1.00 for one book, 50¢ for each additional)	
APPLICABLE TAXES*	$ _____
TOTAL PAYABLE	$ _____
(check or money order—please do not send cash)	

To order, complete this form and send it, along with a check or money order for the total above, payable to Harlequin Books, to: **In the U.S.:** 3010 Walden Avenue, P.O. Box 9047, Buffalo, NY 14269-9047; **In Canada:** P.O. Box 613, Fort Erie, Ontario, L2A 5X3.

Name: _____

Address: _____ City: _____

State/Prov.: _____ Zip/Postal Code: _____

*New York residents remit applicable sales taxes.
 Canadian residents remit applicable GST and provincial taxes.   MTMORDER